A Date with My Boss

Did you know we have an ambiance Spotify playlist for this book?

Scan this code with your Spotify App:

Our books are also available in paperback.

Find our catalog on:
https://cherry-publishing.com/en/

LOLA BLUE

A Date with My Boss

Cherry
Publishing

ISBN: 978-1-80116-776-5

1

Elena

"Are you sure about this?" I asked in a feverish voice.

I've never liked light dresses. And even less so in floral patterns. I look like a hippie on my way to Woodstock, and that's not the point.

"Certain!" laughs Kate. "Have I ever misled you?"

It would take too long to list. So, I cross my arms against my chest and give my best friend a look full of innuendo.

"Well, OK," she admits. "Maybe once or twice..."

As I maintain the eye contact, she grimaces.

"... Six or seven?"

I prefer not to count. Kate is a loyal friend, but when it's about clothes, really, she's about as useful as a square tire.

"Don't exaggerate," she scolds me, finishing off my braid. "You're going to look PERFECT tonight!"

I look in the mirror and wonder what the hell I'm doing here. I arrived in San Francisco just three weeks ago. I moved from the East Coast to the West Coast practically on a whim. Kate pestered me for months to join her, and I finally gave in. She was fed up with me being so far away 'that there's quite a time difference between us!' So, with my literary degree in hand, I decided to cross the United States to find her.

It was a revelation: the sun, the ocean, the way of life, which is so, so, so different! Okay, I'm still in a big city, but it's nothing like New York. And now I find myself in Kate's apartment, getting dressed up like a hippie, because she's developed a hankering for the 1960s since that book she read.

In the mirror, the reflection of my face, which I find far too pale for a city like San Francisco, prompts me to take stock: I'm 24, and I've got all my teeth. That's something. My long chestnut hair is now braided, its natural waves captured in Kate's clever twists. My green eyes are hemmed in with long lashes that I've carefully stretched with black mascara. My make-up remains relatively conservative, and all the better for it.

"That's it! Everyone's going to love it!" exclaims Kate.

I'm not sure about that, but let's face it...

Tonight, we're going to a chic bar. Not only with Kate, but also with Travis, one of my work colleagues. I was thinking more along the lines of staying at my apartment for an evening of reading with a nice hot chocolate and possibly a takeout, but Kate is the type to kick my butt. She was already like that when we were in high school. When I wanted to stay in, she'd practically drag me out by my hair. Well, that's not a bad thing. If I'm honest, it was thanks to her that I met my first boyfriends and had my first intimate experiences. Whether it was at the back of the gym, in the locker-room showers, or in the principal's office during the end-of-year party.

If in life we all have a demon and a little angel resting on our shoulder to tell us what to do, Kate is clearly the demon - but I'm fine with that! I sometimes need her to make decisions that push me out of my comfort zone.

In an hour, we're meeting Travis for our famous evening. The bar is called "El Diablo". Now that's what I call an oddly romantic name.

"Is it Latino?" I ask with a touch of trepidation.

"Absolutely not!"

"Is there a country night then?"

"No... Not at all..."

I pout. I wonder why she's dressing me up like this, if it's not for a theme party. But never mind. I've got to meet my colleagues outside work. They say it's essential for a healthy life. Stuff like drinking, hooking up with guys and so on. Some say it's what makes life worth living. Although I'm usually more the type to hit on fictional guys through the pages of my books, this time I'm letting Kate take my hand.

After all, I owe her that much...

If I've managed to get hired at this great bookstore in the heart of San Francisco, it's thanks to her. She also works there - with Travis, of all people! She warned me: "You'll love him. But don't touch!"

Yeah. There's clearly a purpose behind all this.

I'll probably be the third wheel, but I don't mind. If it means I can show her how grateful I am for this new job and this new life, then I'll gladly watch her smooch.

"Here, I'll take a photo of you for a souvenir," she says, flashing me with her phone.

"No, Kate, don't..."

Without even looking up, she continues:

"You'll see, these parties are always great. There's music, atmosphere..."

3, 2, 1...

"... Guys," she adds, nudging me.

I knew it! It was guaranteed.

"Stop it, you know I'm not looking. I recently broke up with Percy and I have no desire to start up again," I try to justify myself.

"Precisely! To forget the old, there's nothing like a dip in the pool! That's my motto!"

And it rhymes...

I look up at the ceiling. It has to be. What did I expect? She always tries too hard, Kate, that's just the way she is. On the other hand, it's also part of her unparalleled charm. It's also why I follow her so blindly. She always seems sure of herself, she's confident, strong, straight in her boots and when something doesn't please her, she's not shy about pointing it out - usually by screaming.

And then... she pushes me to excel and stands up for me. I remember when Jordan Bernon pulled my hair in junior high school. She came in like a super warrior to kick him in the balls. I thought they were going to come out of his mouth. He turned bluer than a Na'vi[1] and started singing in ten octaves.

We catch a cab and Kate gives us the address, hastily reapplying her lipstick.

"I'm so glad you're here. My best friend! In San Francisco! Finally!"

"Yeah. I can't say it was an easy decision."

A decision made much more credible after Percy decided to dump me. Nothing was really keeping me in New York anymore. My parents are from Connecticut. I could have moved closer to them, but I chose to live my life in Kate's company. My existence, without her, was becoming too boring.

"You're the one who left overnight, though," I add.

"I know, I know, I know. But you have to admit, it was a good idea! Have you seen this place? It's gorgeous!"

It's true that San Francisco isn't bad at all. The city unfolds before me like a mosaic of dreams, each neighborhood exuding a distinct character. The hills undulate beneath a sky that plays with shades of blue, sometimes clear as if washed by the ocean, sometimes dense with mist, creating an almost mystical atmosphere.

As I cab through its streets, I'm captivated by the eclectic

---

1 *Blue character featured in James Cameron's Avatar films.*

10

architecture - pastel Victorian houses sit alongside sleek modern buildings. There's an irresistible charm in this cohabitation of old and new, as if the city embraced its past while looking resolutely to the future.

And all the while, as I observe the magnificence of the city, Kate is powdering her nose. How can she not enjoy this moment?

Streetcars, with their nostalgic tinkling, climb up and down the hills, offering spectacular views of the sparkling bay, where the Golden Gate Bridge stands proudly like a red titan.

But what makes San Francisco unique for me is its atmosphere. Something I'd never experienced before in New York. There's an atmosphere of freedom and openness in the air. People here seem to embrace their differences, whether in the way they dress, speak or live. There's a sense of community, a spirit of 'live and let live' that spreads an invigorating energy through the city. It's true... perhaps it's the ideal place for a fresh start.

"When are you going to show me your apartment, by the way?"

"Tomorrow, if you like."

"Mmh mmh... Tomorrow, I have other plans for you."

I arch an eyebrow quizzically, but Kate waves me off.

I don't really like surprises. Especially when they come from her.

As the cab slows down, my eyes land on the front of 'El Diablo'. The bar immediately stands out in the busy street. The façade is painted a deep, bold red, evoking the color of flames and passion. Black lanterns, suspended on either side of the entrance, cast a subdued light, creating a slightly creepy atmosphere.

What the fuck did I get myself into?

I can't take my eyes off the bar, while Kate, hyperactive, is already paying the fare.

11

Above the door, a large carved wooden panel depicts a smiling devil, his mischievous eyes seemingly following every passer-by. The name 'El Diablo' is written in stylized gold letters, gleaming under the discreet spotlights. And what can I say about the tinted windows, except that they make me want to run for my life?

I leave the cab and the two of us meet in front of the entrance.

"Do you trust me?" asks Kate.

"I... uh..."

Next to the big door, a slate announces special events and bands. Tonight, it's the Metal Cats On Fire.

Suddenly, I'm not so sure...

"Come on. Come on, you coward," my friend sneers.

We walk through the door and immediately I'm overwhelmed by the atmosphere inside the bar. The dark walls, adorned with decorations evoking hell and diabolical folklore, give the place an almost theatrical atmosphere. Small, dark wooden tables, randomly positioned around the room, are lit by candles that cast dancing shadows on customers' faces. Damn, I'm going to pee myself. This place is totally... creepy!

"Do you come here often?"

"I can't hear you over the music. Speak up."

The bar itself is a spectacle in its own right: behind the counter, bottles of all shapes and colors line up on shelves lit by glowing lights, giving the illusion of a blazing fire. The bartender, dressed in a black shirt and red vest, handles the bottles with fascinating dexterity, capturing the attention of those who approach to order. The music, a mixture of rock and metal, vibrates in the air. It's deafening. Screens hanging on the walls broadcast clips that have nothing to do with what's playing.

Kate pulls me by the hand to a vacant table near the stage,

where a band is preparing to play. The low, round table is surrounded by some used but comfortable red leather sofas. She settles in with infectious enthusiasm, while I sit more timidly, absorbing the details of this unique place.

"Where is Travis?" I ask.

"He won't be long."

I'm really looking forward to meeting him. He also works at the bookstore, so we'll be rubbing shoulders. Tomorrow's my first day, and I hope I don't have a massive hangover.

All around us, the bar is buzzing with energy. Groups of friends are laughing and talking loudly, couples are engrossed in intimate conversations, and a few loners seem lost in thought or hypnotized by the music. The air is thick with the scent of beer, whisky and an indefinable blend of spices and perfumes.

And naturally, I'm wondering what the hell I'm doing here.

The incessant buzz of conversation intensifies as new customers arrive, looking for a seat or making their way to the bar. The atmosphere is electric, filled with palpable anticipation for the band about to play.

"Look, they're playing tonight," Kate shouts, pointing to the stage where the members of *Metal Cats On Fire* are starting to set up. "They look pretty crazy, don't they?"

I nod, still overwhelmed by the ambience of the place. On stage, the lights begin to flicker, creating a fascinating interplay of flash and shadow that dances across the shimmering instruments. The band members, dressed in black leather and torn T-shirts, tune their guitars with intense concentration.

"Would you like something to drink?" she asks, leaning towards me to make herself heard.

"Just a soda, maybe."

Kate nods and heads for the bar to order. I find myself alone at the table, watching the people around me.

My eyes roam the room, lingering on the bizarre and captivating details of the decor. Skulls, snakes, pictures of flames and occult symbols adorn the walls, each element adding to the bar's mysterious, creepy aura.

Kate returns with our drinks, a big smile on her face. She sets a soda down in front of me and raises her glass in a silent toast. I raise mine in return, and as our glasses meet in a gentle clink, the band begins to play, filling the bar with raw, intoxicating energy.

I gradually relax, letting myself be carried away by the music and the atmosphere. Maybe this evening won't be so bad after all. Maybe I'll even be able to enjoy myself, despite the strangeness of the place.

Just as this thought crosses my mind, Kate starts screaming, shaking her arms.

As the band launches its first energetic notes, a silhouette makes its way through the crowd towards our table. I can tell it's Travis. Even in the semi-darkness of the bar, his charisma is undeniable. *Wow.* I can see why Kate is after him. Tall and elegantly built, he moves with eye-catching ease. His brown hair, cut short and impeccably styled, frames a face with well-defined features, lit by a confident smile. His deep brown eyes seem to catch and reflect the dim lights of the bar, adding an intriguing sparkle to his allure.

He wears a black shirt, slightly open at the collar, which highlights his tanned complexion and discreet but noticeable musculature. His jeans are fitted, completing a style that is both casual and polished. As he approaches, I notice an elegant watch on his wrist, a subtle contrast to the rough atmosphere of the bar.

"Hello, you two!" he says in a warm, confident voice that can be heard over the music. Sorry for the delay, traffic was hell.

Kate rises to greet him with a friendly hug, while I remain

seated, slightly intimidated by his aura of confidence. He turns to me, his smile widening.

"You must be the new colleague Kate can't stop talking about. Welcome to San Francisco! I'm Travis."

His handshake is firm but warm, and his gaze direct but kind. I immediately feel more at ease, despite the hustle and bustle of the bar and the energy of the band now in full swing.

"Thanks, my name's Elena," I reply, trying to hide my nervousness.

Travis settles down next to us, quickly ordering a beer before turning in our direction, ready to get to know each other better.

"He's being a gentleman, but I've told Travis about you, haven't I!" Kate points out.

"Yeah, that's right. Now I want to know everything," he assures me. "At least, what I don't know yet..."

I bet Kate told him all about me! I feel red as a peony. And it can't be the soda's fault!

"Oh, there's not much to say, really, I..."

"Elena Sanders... You're always far too modest," my friend says. "Well, OK, Travis, I'm going to give you an exposé of who she is, in several points."

"It's really not necessary..."

"Number one: she's a great friend and a bit of a shy girl."

I smile nervously, then sink into my chair as if absorbed by it. It's a good thing the band is playing loud, because Kate is screaming to be heard.

"Number two: she's got everything she needs right where she needs it! And I can vouch for that, because I've already seen her naked!"

She doesn't have to say that.

"Number three: she hasn't had a guy in a while and she wants to get laid!"

It's the moment the musicians have chosen to stop playing, and, of course, all eyes turn to us, because Kate hasn't lowered the sound of her voice.

I feel like liquefying myself. It's horrible.

"Oops. I may have spoken a little loudly."

"Maybe," confirms Travis.

"Hey, you know what? We should take a picture to immortalize this moment: my best friend and my favorite colleague in the same party! I want to cry, I'm so happy! Come on, come on, come closer."

I'll note one thing, though: nobody dressed like a damned hippie, and I'm a bit ridiculous.

I comply with Kate's request and move closer to the two of them. My friend takes the photo, first asking us to look pretty, then to make a face, and finally to smile with all our teeth. We go along with it, and I have to admit I'm enjoying it. It's... kind of fun, actually.

"Well, uh... let's talk about the bookstore, shall we?"

"We don't talk business at night, do we? Right, Travis?"

The young man laughs, then puts his glass back on the table.

"What do you want to know?"

"How's the boss?" I ask.

"Matthew?"

This time, it's Kate who looks dreamy.

"Ah, he's... she begins. He's... how can I put this, uh... a little... a little rough. But frankly, really sexy!"

Travis gives her an amused look.

"Oh yeah? You think he's sexy?"

"You'd have to be blind not to see it!"

I rather expected them to tell me about this 'Matthew' in the context of work, but well...

We continue the evening and I start to get on well with

16

Travis - which makes me feel better. I'd hate to arrive tomorrow and see complete strangers. I've always had trouble forming social relationships. I'm rather reserved in my own way. I tend to be reserved when I know people, so... if I don't know them...

But thanks to Kate, that won't be a problem. Since my friend has already given a broad presentation of myself, I now expect the same from Travis. The more hours go by, the more I learn about him. He's a literature fan too. He honestly doesn't fit the profile. He's a big guy, a fan of gossip and crime novels, but also of personal development. He's got a mouth on him and he's from Tahiti.

Then he spends the rest of the evening talking about the notable differences between life on the islands and in the big cities. And when he's drunk, it seems he's not so kind to San Francisco:

"I'm telling you the truth... It's a very nice place, but it's not as nice as the islands, damn it... I mean... the mentality is so different! Over there, there's more solidarity, you know?"

"I'd love it to be like that here," agrees Kate.

"But that's never going to be the case, because it's a question of culture, I think. Here, we're super individualistic. That's just the way it is. Over there, it's really not the same. Here, I told you about the time..."

And he goes on talking. I listen attentively because it's quite captivating. The islands, his travels, his passion for books and, above all, his dog. Travis is gaga over it! It's like a son to him, and now he's showing us dozens and dozens of photos of it. Kate raves about him, marveling at how much he's grown.

By the time the evening comes to an end, it's around 2 a.m. and I have a feeling that waking up tomorrow won't be easy. I haven't touched a drop of alcohol - because that's not my style - but Kate seems to have overindulged. So, I decide to take her home and sleep there, to make sure she'll be all right - you never know with her!

She takes off her shoes in the hallway and throws them across the room.

"But don't worry... everything's fine! I'm a big f... oops... girl."

"That's right, that's right. You're going to sit quietly in the bedroom, and..."

"Without removing my make-up? You're sick! If I do this tomorrow, I'm gonna look like a... panda. You want to put me in a zoo, don't you?"

Actually, that wouldn't be bad, yeah!

"It's okay, I'll take care of it for you."

As she sits on the edge of the bed, I grab her make-up remover. It's quick and well done.

Once everything is in place, Kate falls asleep like a baby in less time than it takes to say it, and clearly, given the hour, I don't have time to go home. If I don't want to look like hell tomorrow, I'd better get to bed right away.

As I leave the bedroom, I sweep my eyes across the living room and land on the sofa.

I imagine it will do the trick.

In no time at all, after a quick wash, I settle in, hoping that tomorrow will be a good day.

First impressions are always the most important. I can't miss!

* * *

"Wake up, snorer!"

How does Kate manage to look as fresh as the morning dew when it's only 7 a.m. and, a few hours before, she was dead drunk? She seems to have a secret technique, it's not possible otherwise. I think she's a witch. Yes. That's all I see.

"Mmh... Five more minutes..."

"And being late for work? No way! It's your first day, baby!"

Damn... She's right...

With all the difficulty in the world, I extricate myself from my makeshift bed to find her at the small kitchen table. She hands me a coffee - which I gladly grab. In fact, I think I'd like to drink directly from the machine.

"Why do I have a headache even though I haven't had anything to drink?! I feel like I've got a hangover."

"It's because you support me emotionally."

"Not at all," I retort, swallowing my coffee almost in one gulp.

"Wow! A second one?"

I nod hungrily. Oh, hell, yes! I'd make a whole pot. But I'd rather not come to work with muscle spasms.

"Are you ready?" she asks, a big smile on her face.

"Now more than ever."

"All right, then! In that case, get ready, because we'll be back soon!"

Half an hour later, I'm on the warpath and Kate, despite appearances, is on her second aspirin. I tell her it's not recommended, but she doesn't care.

We take public transport to the bookstore and I leave everything to her because, at the moment, I have no idea where we're going.

I let myself be carried along the streets of San Francisco, enjoying the morning sunshine, until I come upon the bookstore. It's right downtown, on a typical street, with colorful facades on all sides. I'm absolutely enchanted, and from the way Kate elbows me in the ribs, I can see it on my face.

"It's a dream come true..." I murmur.

"I'd forgotten what a *nerd* you are with your books."

"Aren't you?"

She shrugs, then puts the key in the lock of the bookstore.

"No more than that. I just sell them, you know. It's a good thing all bartenders aren't alcoholics," retorts my friend.

Sometimes I really wonder how Kate ended up in a job like this without the slightest appetite for books. But hey, I guess she's right.

Everything is so... just as I imagined it would be. This place is splendid. It's far from being a small local bookstore, quite the contrary: this is a quasi-industrial format, but one that has retained the warmth and authenticity of the buildings of yesteryear. Everything here is wood.

"Come on, I'll show you everything you need to see," she says, pulling me along in her wake.

I would have liked a thousand times more to stay and contemplate the appetizing shelves of books calling out to me, but I guess that's for later. Too bad! Kate takes me to the staff room, where she extols the virtues of the comforts here. She shows me, in turn, the armchair, the drinks - and food - dispenser and the table soccer.

"If you type in the right place, on the vending machine, you can get free stuff, look."

"Oh, no, you don't have to..."

Without giving me time to finish my sentence, my friend throws a big punch at the right rear of the machine, which has the miraculous effect of making it drop a packet of Smarties.

Smiling, she offers me one.

OK, noted.

"And er... so... I'm going to meet a superior, or...?"

"Mmh, wait, Smarties in the mouth..."

I wait a few moments until Kate has finished chewing.

"You're not going to meet a superior right away."

"Why's that?" I ask, arching an eyebrow. "Someone has to train me and tell me what to do, right?"

A mischievous smile lights up my friend's face and I don't like it one bit. She points with her index finger.

"No... Seriously?"

"Oh, come on, it'll be fun! I'll teach you all about this place. Matthew's on vacation. He won't be back for two weeks."

And so, until then, Kate will be training me. Okay, I see... Well, I guess it could be worse. I just hope she knows her job well enough. Not that I don't trust her. Far from it. It's just that... I know her.

"By the way, what did your parents say?"

"Oh, well... You know how they can be. They're a little worried, but I told them it was okay, so..."

"I bet you'll be calling them in a panic tonight."

"There's no point if you teach me how to do my job."

Kate spreads her arms, then claps her hands as if to mark the start of a movie scene.

"OK, speaking of which, we're going to have to take care of the opening, and you'll see, it's not all plain sailing. Right now, by default, you're in the thriller department!"

Not bad at all! I think I'm going to like it here.

"Well, we've got a busy schedule today. Especially you, my poor..."

Once again, I'm having trouble keeping up with her. I do hope that on my first day, she won't overload me with work!

Travis bursts into the room and greets us.

"How are you two doing? Recovered from yesterday?"

"Oh, Travis! A little under the weather, but I'm okay. I was just telling Elena that she's gonna have her hands full today... if you know what I mean."

She slips him a wink, but he doesn't catch it right away. He looks too tired for that. Then, suddenly, his eyes light up.

"Ah, yes, of course, I see!"

"Wait a second," I protest, "because I can't see at all. What exactly is going on?"

"Let's just say we've got a surprise for you."

Again, I don't like it at all.

"Is this what you were telling me about yesterday?"

She nods. I know Kate. She wants to talk. I'm sure she does. I know what she's like. When she's like this, the longevity of the secret is hanging by a thread and she's about to tell me everything.

"Okay, spit it out."

"Okay, get your phone out."

Surprised, I comply.

"What's next?"

Without answering, she snatches it out of my hands and opens Tinder. I choke.

What in the world...?

"But... I... I've never installed this app on my phone, or even created an account, I..."

"Relax, I know. You're too uptight for that. I did it for you."

Okay, this time it's clear, I'm gonna kill her. Yeah, I'm gonna kill her. Good thing I'm going to work in the thriller department, that'll teach me how to hide a body!

"You're sick!"

"Not at all. And... I think you've got a lot of *games*. So... you're not going to go gently home tonight, no, no, sweetheart. You're going to have fun! You're in San Francisco now. It's about time you had a little fun in your new life, isn't it?"

I take a deep sigh, then pick up my phone. I shouldn't... I SO shouldn't. And yet... I want to give in to temptation, just the same. It's not a decision I would have made if Kate hadn't interfered. But now I feel like it all came from her, and I feel less guilty responding to all those offers.

"I... well... I'll just have a look, but... if I don't fancy any-one, I won't force myself, will I? I'm not horny either!"

"No, no, it's clear," she laughs. "Don't forget to dress appropriately, eh?"

I look at the photo she used for my profile. It's the one she took when we were still at home, getting ready.

"Is this a joke? The photo makes me look like I'm on my way to a country bar!"

"Don't pout. You look great. Doesn't she, Travis?"

He passes behind my shoulder while changing, to take a look at the photo.

"Ah, uh... Yeah, yeah, really nice."

I hate it.

Well, I guess I have no choice now.

I start my working day in the bookstore, alongside Kate and Travis. The two of them seem really friendly. The thriller section, where I'm assigned, is a labyrinth of mystery and adventure. The tall, imposing shelves are filled with books with intriguing covers, promising suspense and thrills. I immediately feel in my element, surrounded by stories of clever detectives, unsolved crimes and unexpected twists and turns.

I have a feeling I'm going to like it.

Kate gives me a quick orientation tour, highlighting popular authors and new releases. Her enthusiasm for books is infectious, and I find myself engrossed in the titles she shows me.

"You'll love it here," she says with a wink. "The customers are great, and there's always something new and exciting to read. And since I know you like this genre, I've put you on this shelf for the time being."

She's nice, though. And more interested in books than I thought!

Travis passes by, carrying a stack of books to put away. He stops for a moment to greet us.

"Good first day, Elena?" he asks me with a friendly smile.

"Yes, it's great. There's so much to discover," I reply, looking around in admiration.

The atmosphere in the bookstore is warm and welcoming. Soft lights illuminate the aisles, and the subtle scent of paper and ink wafts through the air. From time to time, a customer approaches to ask for a recommendation or to locate a book, and I try to answer their questions with Kate's help. At the moment, she's supporting me, and I'm mostly assisting her. But in her own words, "the way you're learning, I'm worried about my job".

Suddenly, a notification on my phone catches my attention. *Don't tell me that...*

Yes, it is! Of course. I'm so intimidated, my head's buzzing. It's definitely a Tinder match, which I wasn't expecting at all. I quickly consult all the others and, to be honest, all I see are heavies I don't want to meet at all. But this 'Anderson' seems different.

His photos exude an aura of cool nonchalance, typical of a Californian surfer. Anderson's blond, medium-length hair, wavy with ocean salt, falls carelessly over his forehead. His smile is disarming, revealing perfectly aligned teeth and a glint of mischief in his clear blue eyes, like the ocean on a sunny day.

Don't crack.

His tanned skin speaks of days spent on the beaches of San Francisco, and his body is athletic, but not overly muscular, just enough to guess that he spends a lot of time enjoying outdoor activities. In one of his photos, he holds a surfboard under his arm, with a sunset in the background, reinforcing the image of the perfect surfer.

No, seriously, don't crack up...

In his description, Anderson talks passionately about travel, indie music, and his quest for the best taco in town. He comes across as adventurous, but also unexpectedly profound as he talks about his favorite reads and his love of photography.

Fuck, I'm gonna crack.

There's something refreshingly authentic about the way he presents himself. No forced poses or clichéd quotes. Just a sincere smile, a look that seems to see beyond the lens, capturing a moment of pure happiness.

As I scroll through his photos, I feel a thrill of excitement. Anderson is not only incredibly attractive, he also exudes a warmth and authenticity that makes me want to get to know him.

I press to validate the match.

Damn, I've cracked!

"How are you?" asks Kate.

I jump. Is she a ninja or what? I've got to keep calm. She can't know I've just validated a match; otherwise I'll be hearing about it all day long.

I tuck my phone away in my pocket with the discretion of an elephant trying to skate.

The look she gives me is worth all the remarks in the world.

"It's not what you..."

"Think so? I think it is. That's exactly what I think, isn't it?"

"Yes..."

She lets go of the pile of books she was putting away, then hugs me, laughing.

"Finally, my best friend is going to get laid!"

"Shh, it's okay! Stop it! Stop it! Are you trying to embarrass me or something?"

"There's no shame in that!"

I see a grandmother off to the side, looking at us with a bewildered expression, and I immediately apologize.

"Uh... sorry about my friend, she's... she's a little..."

"Your friend is right. And I'll buy the latest Stephen King."

It's great. Even the grannies are getting in on the act.

So, inevitably, at lunchtime, in the staff room, Travis and Kate keep asking me for details about tonight's game. Except that I have no desire to give them any. So, they come up with their little theories. They're as thick as thieves.

"I'm sure he's a huge weed smoker. With the photo, he figured you were a hippie, and he could get high with you," laughs Kate.

"Whose fault is that, eh?"

"No, no, I've got something better," continues Travis. "I think he's going to take her to an underground music festival to get some magic pills."

They're a pain in the ass.

"None of the above! She doesn't seem the type."

"Can't you at least give us a clue?" complains my friend.

Travis takes a big bite out of his sandwich, then adds to Kate's argument:

"Yeah, because right now, we don't know anything at all."

"How much is it?"

"A what? How much of what?"

Kate lets out a deep sigh.

"Don't you remember our game? It was in high school. Make an effort!"

Ah, now I remember! When Kate and I were in high school, we used to play the game of rating guys out of 10. At first, the grade was based solely on looks, then, as we got to know them, we'd judge their personality too - which was often when the average dropped drastically.

"Physically?"

"Of course, physically! You don't know him yet! What do you think?"

This time, it's my turn to stretch a smile across my lips, because I'm going to make her want it so bad, her teeth will be scraping the floor in two minutes.

"An eleven."

She places both hands on the table, then looks at me intently.

"Are you kidding? It's a really special case, then."

"I know."

"Careful, Elena, we don't give the 'eleven' lightly!" she exclaims.

Laconically, I nod, while Travis looks completely lost. From time to time, he raises an eyebrow to show his incomprehension, then goes on with his meal.

"Right, then. I'll have to get you ready, then."

"N..."

"No! You don't talk! The last 'eleven' we saw in our lives was Logan Hafner, and now he's in the movies. So, it's no small matter, OK? I. Will. Get. You. Ready," she details.

When she's like that, there's no point in trying to reason with her. There's absolutely no point. I know how stubborn she can be when she gets down to it.

"Instead of minding my business, wouldn't you two be better off minding your own?"

They exchange incredulous glances.

"What do you mean?" asks Travis.

Just then, Kate glares at me and kicks me under the table. I grimace, then fall silent.

"She doesn't mean anything. Don't worry, Travis."

"Yes, I... er... I was talking about the gossip in the bookstore. That's why I'm here."

Travis's eye twitches at the thought. He looks at me with an air of mystery.

"In fact, there's some gossip floating around, yeah. But since you don't know anybody, I don't know how relevant it is."

"Swing anyway."

Really, what? I'm always up for a good gossip, me!

"Matthew and Betty split up almost a year ago, but I hear she's still hanging around him.

Well, I admit that doesn't do me much good.

"He doesn't know how to tell a story," resumes Kate. "Betty, she's the kind... See the white witch in Narnia[2] ? Well, that's her. A kind of bitch with platinum blond hair and a heart of ice. She's our general manager. The big boss. And Matthew is our superior. He's pretty nice, generally speaking."

"But he's gone on vacation, right?"

Kate nods.

Okay, I'll know when I see Betty and Matthew, I guess. There seems to be a lot of gossip around here!

Once the day's work was done, I tried to sneak out so Kate wouldn't be on my back, but I didn't count on her eagle eye.

"You're not getting away with this, sweetheart. Come on, baby. Come on."

Damn...

---

2 *American film series based on Narnia novels by writer C. S. Lewis.*

2

Elena

I've got so much make-up on my face; I feel like bozo the clown.

"Am I going to host a birthday party at McDonald's, or am I going on a date right now?" I protest.

"Stop complaining. You're going to be perfect! If it's an 'eleven', you must be a femme fatale!"

I look up at the ceiling.

"But I'm not even going to see him again."

"That's just it! You won't have time to find out if he's an idiot. We both know why you're going on this date, don't we?"

It's all right, you don't have to hammer it so hard. For once, I'm allowing myself to have a little fun. I'm hoping for a lively evening with no tomorrow. Since I've been dumped, long relationships aren't for me. Then I have to take the time to have a bit of fun before I find the right one. The problem is that after a few weeks, you can already see the other person's flaws, and boredom creeps in too.

It's exhausting.

Keeping the flame burning isn't easy.

Every time I ask my parents how they managed to stay together, they seem as surprised as I am, to tell you the truth. It's not particularly encouraging. One day, my mother shrugged, then said: "Well, you were there, so...".

Delighted to have been the cement in their relationship.

I slip on a black dress with a relatively plunging neckline, over which I slip a jacket that belongs to Kate. Leather, a little rock... Not usually my style, but I have to say that it goes pretty well with the rest of the outfit.

"Oh, I put something in the pocket," she smiles.

"Let me guess, it's a condom?"

The smile she gives me means absolutely everything. Sometimes she exasperates me. I reach into my pocket and pull out not one, but three condoms.

"Three?!"

"Different sizes," she retorts as if it's only natural. "Hey, you never know. You might come across an asparagus, a banana, an eggplant, a cucumber..."

"I get it, I get it, stop explaining..."

Pffiouh.

She's impossible, honestly.

It's amazing to be so obsessed. But I'm not going to be picky so I keep the condoms. We both know very well why I'm going there tonight, and it's not to play Scrabble. I want to meet someone and have a good time. I'd like to make it clear that this would never have happened if I hadn't come across Anderson. He really is an 'eleven' and that's why I'm so serious about it. Otherwise, it wouldn't be happening!

"I think you're all set," says Kate. "Ah, it's crazy... They grow up so fast..."

"Shut up."

★ ★ ★

I board the streetcar, my heart pounding with excitement and nervousness. The city lights begin to twinkle as the sun sets, painting the sky in shades of pink and orange. The streets of San Francisco come alive with a nocturnal energy, each neighborhood revealing its unique character under the city lights. A thrill runs through me. It's so exhilarating to do this: just what I want, when I want it. I didn't allow myself so much freedom in New York. Here, I feel all the more like an anonymous person deciding to live the life she wants.

The streetcar winds its way through the city, offering panoramic views of rolling hills, Victorian buildings with colorful facades and bustling streets. I see groups of people heading for restaurants or bars, laughing, couples strolling hand in hand, and street performers starting their nightly shows to applause, 'ohs' and 'ahs'.

As I approach the bar where I'm to meet Anderson, excitement builds inside me. The image of Anderson, with his blond hair and disarming smile, floats before my eyes, and I wonder if he'll be as attractive in person.

* *On the road?*

It's him.

* *I'm coming*

* *I'm already here*

He accompanies his message with a photo of a cocktail that, my goodness, looks delicious.

The streetcar slows down and I get off. My footsteps echo on the sidewalk. The bar sign, a few steps away, shines like a beacon in the dawning night. I adjust my outfit one last time, take a deep breath and head for the entrance.

Come on, cheer up, Elena.

As I enter the bar, I leave the setting sun behind and prepare to meet Anderson. My mysterious surfer.

I weave between the tables, trying to look confident, when a voice draws me out of my musings:

"Elena?"

I suddenly freeze, then turn to discover Anderson.

There he is, standing just a few steps away, and he exceeds all my expectations. Anderson is even more handsome than in his Tinder photos. His lightly tousled blond hair gives him a casual, natural look. His blue eyes, shining under the dim lights of the bar, stare at me with a mixture of curiosity and enthusiasm.

He wears a simple t-shirt, slightly shaping his athletic torso, and jeans that emphasize his slim figure. His look is that of a surfer who's swapped his board for a night on the town, retaining his trademark laid-back aura. A sincere smile lights up his face as he approaches me.

"Hi, it's a pleasure to meet you," he says in a warm voice that seems to make the air around us vibrate.

He holds out his hand, and as I shake it, I feel an immediate connection. His handshake is firm but gentle, and his eyes never leave mine.

I stammer out a reply, overwhelmed by the natural charm he exudes. Anderson is the kind of person who captures attention effortlessly, his presence both soothing and electrifying.

"I hope you didn't wait too long," I stammer, trying to regain my composure.

Soldier down. Soldier down. Mayday! He's so handsome!

"Not at all, I've just arrived. Come on, I've found a quiet corner for us," he replies, guiding me to a secluded table.

Walking alongside him, I can feel the stares of the other customers on us. Anderson, with his confident gait and California surfer aura, seems perfectly in place, and for the first time in a long time, I feel like I'm exactly where I'm supposed to be.

How good it is to change one's life!...

When we sit down, I'm particularly intimidated, but I try not to let on. I mustn't look like a scared kitten if I want him to take me seriously. Okay, I have to drop a joke, something, to show him that I'm not impressed. We're not starting out on an equal footing and he knows it. This guy isn't just handsome. He KNOWS he's incredibly sexy. It's not fair!

The smile he gives me is... devastating.

"Looking at your photo, I expected you to arrive like a hippie, in a *peace and love* van. I kind of liked it."

OK, Touché.

Thanks, Kate! Thanks to her, I feel like I'm going to have a hell of a reputation.

Anderson doesn't seem to have his tongue in his pocket, and I like that.

I'm a little taken aback by his jab, but I don't take offense.

"To tell you the truth, when I showed your photo to some friends, everyone agreed to give you a nickname," he continues.

"Oh yes, which one?"

"Woodstock."

Damn, I was sure this was a bad idea, that outfit last night. She could have taken a more advantageous photo of me!

"I'm sure you're making it up," I retort, lacking a response.

At the same time, the bartender brings us two cocktail glasses. He's already ordered?!

"I've taken a few initiatives," he confirms, as if he's read my mind. "And, about the nickname... um... yes, maybe I'm making it up. But I think it suits you."

I need a comeback. Now. Right now. It's a matter of survival. I don't want him to find me boring. That would be the worst thing possible!

"So, what do you do for a living, apart from catch the wave?"

Anderson stretches a mischievous smile, then stirs the straw in his glass.

"I'm not talking about work. Sorry about that."

"I imagine the same applies to me."

"I don't want to have the upset on my mind tonight. Let's just think about the positive, okay? We're here, together, and this bar is great."

It's true that he's nice. I glance around, soaking up the atmosphere. The bar mixes industrial and chic, with its brick walls. Black metal pendant lights project geometric patterns onto the tables, creating an intimate, artistic atmosphere. Hanging green plants and brightly colored abstract paintings contrast with the rawness of the decor, adding a touch of life and color. The music, a subtle blend of modern jazz and soul, floats in the air, soft enough to allow easy conversation. I'd have much preferred this to 'El Diablo'!

"Cool place, huh?" adds Anderson.

"Not bad, yes."

"It's one of my favorite spots. I like to come here to relax, especially after a long day. Wait, I just hit it, but... did you say 'not bad'?"

I nod, feeling increasingly at ease.

I have a feeling he took it as a dig, so I'm okay with that. My surfer starts laughing and runs a hand through his hair.

"It's clearly the best bar in town," he says with an exaggerated air of offense. "It's more than just... 'not bad'!"

"What's said is said," I retort with a shrug.

The soft light from the bar illuminates her face, accentuating her features and enhancing her natural charm.

"That's the best part."

"I can feel you're about to tell me that you know the owner

well and that he's even a friend of yours," I tease. "It's always the same with bar and restaurant recommendations."

"So, frankly, I think you're exaggerating. Paul is a good mate, no more. Not a close friend."

This comment makes me burst out laughing, but I think that was the intention.

"You're kidding, right?" I ask.

"Of course I do, what do you expect? The boss's name is Joe."

He's hilarious and really handsome. When he laughs, I can see his row of white teeth sparkle.

We continue the evening in the same vein: laughing about everything, remaking the world and, above all, not talking about work. Anderson is so cute... I even find myself dashing out onto the dance floor at one point to enjoy it with him. If I didn't have three or four - or five - drinks up my nose, I don't think I'd even be thinking about it. I'm not that kind of girl. Not at all.

But with him, everything's different and I let myself be tempted. And at the stroke of 2 a.m., we're practically the last customers in the bar, which is about to close. I approach the counter, but Anderson seems determined to pay.

No way! I don't want to be indebted to him!

I reach into my pocket and hand the change to the bartender, who looks at me incredulously.

"Ma'am, we don't take... condoms for change."

I sober up in one go.

"Oh, for fuck's sake! Uh... sorry, I... I... by card, it's... it's maybe better, so, I..."

Anderson, once again, bursts out laughing. But this time, I understand that he's interested and that the evening may not be ready to end. In the end, this incident isn't a bad thing.

"Leave it," he says. "I'm inviting you in. It's my pleasure."

I resign myself. Crap. This is a real shame. I feel like becoming the broken glass the waiter is picking up to put in the garbage can. I try - vainly - to summon up some courage, so as not to liquefy.

We leave the bar and once again Anderson teases me:

"I see you had another idea in mind."

"Don't get me wrong."

"Oh, sorry," he scoffs, raising his arms in peace. "I didn't know condoms were common currency in San Francisco."

"So er..."

"Then I'll take you home. Let's go."

Anderson doesn't leave me much choice, and to tell you the truth, that's fine with me. I don't want to have to look for a cab at this hour of the morning - because let's face it, as far as public transport is concerned, I've had it! So, I follow him without resisting.

And then I fall under his spell: he stops in front of a beautiful 1966 Ford Mustang, red and maintained as if it were new.

Now that's a man of taste.

"Do you like it?" he asks as I stall on the car.

"Rather, yes."

"Are you still going to say that it's 'not bad', Woodstock?"

"My name is Elena."

"I prefer Woodstock. I'm sorry. I just... I think it's cuter."

Why am I so attracted to this guy? If I'm so accommodating, it's probably largely thanks to the condoms in my pocket that remind me of the purpose of this date. But also because let's face it: he's awfully good-looking. To spit on an opportunity like this would be an infamy that no woman on earth would forgive me.

The handsome blond takes off. The car purrs like a lion and I shudder.

"Still 'not bad'?" he teases me.

"It changes to 'nice'."

And instead of being offended, Anderson seems to enjoy it.

He walks me back to my apartment. That's rather charming of him. I feel comfortable in his car. It's comfortable and it's been a long time, anyway, since I've had such a pleasant date. Last time, the guy tried to shove his tongue straight into my mouth without going through the exchange stage first. I pushed him away and left, swallowing three pieces of gum.

Since the streets are almost deserted at this hour, he doesn't hesitate to step on the gas - probably to show me off, and I have to say it works!

I point him in the right direction, and, at the same time, we strike up another conversation about this town.

"Are you new here?"

"Not at all. I'm from San Francisco. I couldn't live without this city."

He stops just outside my house, then turns off the ignition.

"It's here," he says. "You've arrived, Woodstock."

Kate... I'm really going to kill you.

"Thank you."

Come on, damn it, be brave.

I don't feel like getting out of his car at all, but he doesn't seem insistent. Yet his gaze settles on me with desire. I can feel it from here. That said, Anderson is a good man, and I don't think this is entirely what he's looking for.

Push it, you idiot!

I feel like Kate is talking in my head! It's so frustrating to leave it at that.

"Is something wrong? Forgot your flower crown or your joint?"

Instead of laughing, I lean towards him in a movement of tenderness and without giving him time to answer anything, I place a kiss on his lips.

That's always a bit scary. Kate has several sayings and one of them is: 'A kiss that lasts more than five seconds has a good chance of going doggy-style.'

Charming, eh!

But maybe that's what I want.

1... 2... 3...

New life, new woman. New habits. I want to have fun too.

4...

And Anderson's crotch won't say otherwise.

5...

This is it, the fateful moment. This is when it's all supposed to go to hell.

Damn it! For once, Kate was right!

Anderson doesn't want to leave it at that, and that's fine with me, but this time he's the one taking the lead.

In the car, it's not necessarily the most comfortable place in the world, but neither of us really cares at this moment. All that matters is the present and the urgency I feel at my fingertips.

I undress him as best I can and he does the same, with the wild haste of two beings irrevocably attracted to each other. Anderson devours me with his kisses, and every time he runs his tongue over mine, he awakens millions of sensations in me that I want to explore with him. His skin is endlessly soft and warm.

When he grabs me and positions me astride him, I let out a slight cry of surprise, which he laughs at.

"What's going on, Woodstock? You weren't expecting this?"

"You know I did."

In the cockpit, the temperature rises another notch. And as our foreplay gets hotter, it's my initiative to take the condoms out of my pocket.

"What size?" I ask.

"Your guess is as good as mine."

"You really want me to start experimenting."

"Maybe yes."

Her smile is absolutely irresistible. You'd have to be made of marble not to fall for his dimples and his eyes. I'm sure this guy was tailor-made by a god from Olympus but sent to earth three thousand years too late.

In this case, since the gentleman asks, I take on the task with a deftness that doesn't displease him, and once the right size has been found, the serious business can begin.

In a concert of sighs, caresses and kisses, I'm swept up in a whirlwind of emotions that leave me stunned.

Damn.

The question of whether my pleasure comes from his skill or from my time of abstinence crosses my mind, but I can't be that dishonest. I've already had a few experiences and none of them comes close to Anderson's level. When I spoke of the god of Olympus, I wasn't so far from the truth after all. It's hardly surprising when you see how hard he works and how fiery he is. Even the car windows were fogging up, as if they were trying to hide us. I've never done it in a car, like this, in the middle of the street. Fortunately, I live in a quiet neighborhood and my neighbors are mostly old folks. Otherwise, there'd be a lot of gossip.

We both finish in a sweat, but full of pleasure, and as I sink back into the passenger seat, Anderson gives me a lustful look.

"I'm going to regret that it's only for one night, Woodstock."

Me too. But that's what I promised myself: one date.

"I'm not ready for a relationship, Mustang."

He smiles. The reference to the model of his car seems to amuse him.

"Difficult breakup?"

"Is it okay to talk about this on a Tinder date?

Especially after fucking...

He shrugs as he zippers up his pants.

"Why not?"

"Yes, a little. I wanted to mark the occasion and havesome fun.

"Successful?" he asks, raising an eyebrow.

"Rather, yes."

I smile frankly. I had a great time and for a few hours I forgot everything else. So, it was a success. At least as far as I'm concerned. But one question remains unanswered.

"What about you? What were you looking for?"

As if to avoid the answer, he runs a hand through his hair with an evasive air.

"A bit of fun, actually. I spent too much time becoming someone I wasn't. It's been a real ordeal. So, now, I'm trying to get on with my life."

"Oh, poor Mustang, did you have an overbearing mother?"

My remark at least had the merit of triggering a great burst of laughter in him.

"Come on, Woodstock. You're working tomorrow, right?"

I nod. I didn't want this moment to end, because the sorry look he's giving me means we'll never see each other again.

San Francisco is a huge city, and the chances of running into each other again are slim to none.

No, what am I talking about? I don't want to meet him again! This is a one-night stand!

That's how you heal, they say. Usually, when I'm in pain somewhere, I prefer the drug route to the penile route, but why not? I've got nothing against alternative medicine. Especially when the area concerned is none other than the heart.

It's still in tatters and that won't change for the time being.

I leave Anderson's car and return to my apartment. Half-drunk, but still troubled by this memorable evening, I crawl into bed, trying to chase Mustang's wonderful eyes from my mind.

3

Matthew

"Your turn, Matt."

The sun is high in the sky, the wind is blowing and I'm more than happy to take on the challenge. When it comes to doing something stupid where you put yourself unnecessarily at risk, you can always count on me to keep going.

Yeah, the wave is huge, but it doesn't scare me.

I go for it, stand up with a jerk on my board and glide with an ease that impresses everyone else. The air is pure, as is the sensation. This freedom is incomparable. It's nothing like what I experience on the job.

"Wow, you really nailed it," says Derek.

"You bastard. You could go pro," laments Anton.

Both jealous!

"Look at these two idiots," I scoff. They defy the master and think they can get away with it.

They both burst out laughing and pat me on the back. The best thing about this beach is the shack that sells cold drinks and hot dogs. Ah, and then there are the waves, too.

I grab my board with both hands, then head over to the small establishment to order with the two dumbasses.

We've been scouring the best spots on the coast for several weeks now, and I have to say it's a rest that does me a world of good.

The good thing about these two is that I can always count on them. Over the last few weeks, they've been with me as I've toured every rock festival I could. It's been absolutely relaxing, and I might as well say it straight away: I've no desire to get back to work. It's not that I'm a slacker, far from it, it's just that...

"How are things going with your ex?" asks Derek, opening his beer.

Son of a bitch. He knows very well that this is a sensitive subject.

"I don't feel like talking about it at all."

"Oh, come on, Anton and I call you 'ideal son-in-law' now."

"Shut up, you morons."

"Remember the time he invited us to his 'barbecue'? There were waiters."

I shake my head and smile, even though deep down I'm a little ashamed of myself.

Fuck, when I think about it, that relationship was really devastating. Little by little, without my realizing it, she had taken possession of me and everything I was. I no longer looked like myself. One day, I got up and looked in the mirror at a guy I didn't recognize. I was shocked and realized I had to run. Away. That I had to leave for new horizons. That's why I bought my van back.

"You're idiots. You'll walk home."

"No, no, it's okay... It was a good barbecue," laughs Anton. "Come on, please, my legs are already aching."

Hilarious, we find my van and settle in. These two idiots like to call it the 'Mystery Machine', because the vehicle re-sembles the one in Scooby-Doo[3] . What they don't know is

---

3 *American franchise comprising numerous series, TV movies and animated films created by Hanna-Barbera Studios.*

the dream this van represents, for me. Putting money aside, restoring it until it's capable of going more than a hundred kilometers before breaking down, that's really something.

I could cruise the coasts and escape the reality that imprisons me. That's all I want, but for now... I'm staying here. On the outskirts of this city that's suffocating me. At least I've got two friends to accompany me through thick and thin.

"When are you going back to work?" asks Anton, as if I wanted to broach the subject.

"You know you're getting out of the van, right?"

"You've changed, man!" says Derek.

"What now?"

"You didn't even take the number of the girl who was checking you out on the beach."

Oh, this?

"I'll leave it with you. I'm a sharing kind of guy. With a bit of luck, if you follow me closely, you might be able to catch a fish or two in your life."

I start the van, leaving behind the sound of the waves and the laughter of my friends. Driving along the coastal road is therapeutic, the magnificent views of the ocean and cliffs allow me to clear my head. Derek and Anton continue to joke and laugh, but my thoughts wander elsewhere.

I think about my ex. Damn it, I don't want to see her that bad...

"Matt, are you with us?"

Anton pulls me out of my thoughts.

"Yeah, yeah, I was just thinking about something," I reply.

"About that witch who's ruining your life, eh?"

Derek seems to read my mind.

I sigh. Maybe it's time for a change. I can't go on like this. It's not an option. I'll break eventually.

"I think I'll dot the i's and cross the t's."

"Ha! I knew our Matt hadn't totally disappeared!" exclaims Derek, giving me a friendly pat on the shoulder.

"If she's a pain, give me a call," says Anton. "If I can help in any way..."

I smile at their comments. They're stupid, but I like them that way. I wouldn't want them to change for the world.

★ ★ ★

I lie in bed at night, thinking about it all and looking back. How could she have broken me so?

Last week, it was Marina. The week before that, Jade. Before that, it was Francesca. I can't say I've ever limited myself when it comes to dating. There was never a tomorrow. Always one-night stands, or a few days at the most. After what happened to me with that damn ex-girlfriend, I have no desire to get back into a long-term relationship. I'm not ready to settle down. I was, but she ruined everything. She made me everything I'm not and I've come to hate myself sometimes.

I got scared.

I ran away.

I became aware of her crazy manipulative temperament. It was too much for me. Sometimes, running away is still the best solution. When I was younger, I had dreams and they were very different. Today, I'm in the process of making them come true. My deepest aspiration is freedom. It's what everyone should be entitled to, and with her, it wasn't possible. Her dreams always came before mine, and it took me a long time to admit that the two of us weren't right for each other. That's just the way it is. Sometimes it takes time to realize certain truths. Even more so if they're painful.

I remember that day like it was yesterday. It was then that I realized that something was wrong and that I didn't belong among all those people. We had decided to organize a barbecue. I expected it to be convivial, but it was quite the opposite. And I wanted to invite Anton and Derek.

"Oh, honey... no..." she said, sounding sweet.

She touched my face, then placed a kiss on my cheek.

"We can't make them come."

"Why?" I asked.

She swept the assembly with her eyes. Inside was her family. Nothing but her family. Even mine had been excluded and, little by little, she was separating me from my friends and all relationships that didn't concern her. She wanted to be at the center of my life and control it in its entirety. But still, Anton and Derek...

"Because they're not... well... how can I put this... look around you."

I did. As if I was going to find a real answer. Of course, I didn't. All I saw were people dressed as if they were on their way to church, waiters filling champagne glasses or wine glasses and... that was it.

That's when it hit me.

I didn't give a damn about the nice barbecue, the waiters, the neatly mown lawn, her chic parents who saw me as some kind of crazy hippie with a passion for surfing. Like a nice doggie who goes into his kennel when you ask him to. I didn't give a damn about the SUV, the margaritas or the little turtleneck sweater.

It wasn't me and I was suffocating.

"I need to get out," I said.

And that's what I did.

When I got back once the guests had left, we had the time of our lives. It was a real storm in the house. And every time, the problem was me. Always me. As if I wasn't good enough for her. Oh, yes, she made me feel that. She kept reminding me, in her gestures, in her tone, in her words, that I was lucky she was looking at me and not the other way around.

And all that was left of my former life was my surfboard, rotting in the corner of the garage.

That evening, I went out once more and saw Anton and Derek, who were at the bar, playing pool. They hadn't seen me in ages, and from the looks on their faces, I knew I had to run. I was white as a sheet, changed, without an ounce of personality left.

But at that moment, a spark deep inside me took over again. Like a life force. An inner current that forbade me to let myself die. It screamed in my heart that I had so much more to live for than this life of hell and conformity.

That evening, I decided to drop everything and start afresh.

4

Elena

"Give me more! No, seriously, you're a real cheapskate, Elena!" says Kate with a look of outrage.

Details, details... She's a funny one! It's not like I want to spill my guts like that!

But then, in the break room, she and Travis look like they're just waiting. They're like two hungry dogs at the sight of a bone to gnaw. Hanging on my every word, all they want to know is the gritty, embarrassing details of last night's date.

"Sorry for you weirdos, but I've got nothing more to say to you."

"Now that's just nasty! But I'm sure I can find a way to make you talk."

"No way," I said, crossing my arms.

"That's what you think."

She gets up from the table and walks over to me.

What's she still thinking, that twisted woman? Whenever she's like this, I'm wary of her like the plague.

"Get her, Travis!"

He does so at full speed, then grabs my arms, while she rummages in the pocket of the jacket I'm still wearing. What the hell is she...? Oh, I get it, damn it!

"Ah ah!" she exclaims. "I knew it! Only two condoms! But

there were three yesterday. So, you're going to have to confess. Something's happened! There was coitus! And you won't tell me?"

OK, I'm unmasked and also forced to admit that Kate-Lock Holmes is pretty good at her field investigations.

"Hey, wait a minute," she continues, "it's the large size that's been used..."

"All right, stop!" I cut her off. "I'll... I'll give you some details. But, really, does Travis have to be here?"

He raises his hands in peace, then heads for the door.

"I understand. Private discussion. Anyway, my break's over. See you later, girls!"

Once he's gone, Kate turns to me with a charmed air:

"Don't you think he's cute?"

"Yeah, especially when you use it as a hunting dog to attack me."

"Well, come on," she continues, walking over to the machine to give it a whack. "Tell me about it."

She picks up her pack of M&M's, grumbling because she wanted a Snicker, then positions herself opposite me, hanging on my lips.

"I don't want to be too... touchy-feely, you know. Especially since we did it somewhere unexpected, so..."

"Unexpected? Oh, wow, that's even better! I love it. So go ahead, unpack."

"In his car."

There, she opens her eyes wide, like a fish in a vat of ice before being sold at the market.

"You've got to be kidding me! Oh, what a slut! You're not ashamed of yourself."

Smiling, I say:

"It wasn't! And, boy, was it well put together. I'm not telling you!"

"I'm so jealous. I had a much less fun night, if you must know. I finished my favorite show, Travis wasn't available to grab a bite to eat with me."

"Why don't you just tell him you're really into him?"

"What's wrong with you? You don't try to catch game by running at it like a savage."

She's the best! Kate is the queen of the wilderness when it comes to men. She's no slouch, and most of them tend to flee when she gets her spear out. I think only the most adventurous stay with her. It doesn't surprise me, for the moment, that no one has put a ring on her finger.

To think I was supposed to have a ring on MY finger...

"All right, all right, I see. I'll keep quiet."

"You'd better. But not too much, because the big bosses want to see you in their offices. You'll have to talk, won't you?"

I'm speechless, my eyes wide open.

"Bosses? But why? What do you think it's about?"

Kate shrugs, her expression a mixture of amusement and curiosity.

"No idea. Maybe they want to congratulate you on a job well done? Or maybe they've discovered that you've been fooling around in a stranger's car and want to give you a medal for your bravery."

I give her a dark look, but she just laughs.

"Go see what they want. And then come and tell me all about it, eh?"

I get up, a little nervous. As I walk to the bosses' office, I think back to my evening with Anderson. I have a goofy grin on my face. It's been unexpected, crazy, but incredibly exciting. I really wonder what he does for a living. He probably runs a gym, the way he looks. Or maybe he's a millionaire serial lover with a string of conquests, like in the books.

Arriving at the office door, I take a deep breath and knock.

"Come in!"

I open the door, and there's the principal, Mrs. McGee. She's not alone. She's accompanied by a young blond man who looks like a business school graduate.

So that's her, Betty...

Betty McGee embodies a cold, bourgeois elegance. Barely older than me, she's a well-groomed beauty with perfectly coifed blond bob hair and coolly analytical light-blue eyes. Her tailored pantsuit emphasizes her slender figure, complemented by designer high heels and discreet luxury jewelry. Her presence is both intimidating and fascinating, reflecting undeniable self-confidence and professionalism.

I don't really know what to say to her face. I immediately feel like I'm dressed like garbage and she's really undermining my morale right now.

"You... you wanted to see me?"

"Yes. I'm told you've recently been hired. Everything's been put in order, which is great. How are things going?"

I was expecting anything but this question. So, I freeze for a moment.

"Uh... well... yes? It's alright. I... I really like books, you know."

Her blue eyes pierce me. It's as if she can read my mind. It's both disturbing and unpleasant.

"Wonderful. I have a special mission for you. It's also my way of welcoming you. I like it when teams mix and consolidate."

I open my eyes wide. A mission? I... I didn't expect it to go so fast. I haven't been here very long! Betty McGee, her expression always impeccably controlled, slides a folder onto the table in front of me.

"We're organizing a major literary event. This is an opportunity for you to demonstrate your skills. You will work closely with your superior. He is our events manager. You'll find all the details you need in this folder."

I pick up the folder, my hands trembling slightly. A literary event? Sounds like quite a challenge, especially for a new employee like me.

"Your manager will guide you, but I expect you to show initiative and innovation. This experience will be beneficial to your professional development," she says, with a hint of encouragement in her icy voice.

"I'll... I'll do my best," I murmur.

"Perfect. You can start right now. Let me introduce you to your direct superior."

I nod, still a little in shock, then get up to leave the office. As I walk towards the office of this manager I don't know, I feel a lump of nervousness in my stomach. This is an incredible opportunity, but also a huge responsibility. I take a deep breath, reminding myself that it's opportunities like this that shape a career.

Since this is the first time I'm going to meet him, Betty accompanies me, to avoid any unpleasantness that may follow. I can't pretend to be fully confident. That would be a lie. In fact, I'm quite intimidated by my boss. She doesn't seem to be very accommodating, and what I thought was a fairly quiet bookstore is actually run by a businesswoman with the look of an icy beauty. I can't believe it! I saw a quantity of files on her desk that was truly... astronomical. Not to mention the one she slipped me.

At the moment, I don't dare leaf through it. Would this be a good idea? Would she see it as taking the initiative? No, I don't think so...

She knocks three times on an office door, then enters. The bookstore really isn't laid out the way I'd imagined it. So, OK, there's our floor, where, simple employees that we are, we toil away carrying lives, shelving them and manning the till. But there's another, much more 'start-up', 'corporate' side to this bookstore: its top floor. That's where the offices are, and as Betty tells me how she runs the place, the dream of the little neighborhood bookstore is shattered. Let's face it - and rightly so - Betty is in it to make money, not for the love of reading. Well, maybe she does, I don't know, but I don't get the feeling I'm looking at someone who's passionate about reading.

She seems in a hurry, disillusioned and rather annoyed - under any circumstances.

As she pushes open the door, my eyes lock with those of my supervisor and my heart stops dead: Anderson.

"Meet Matthew Anderson, your supervisor. Matt', can I leave you to deal with the new girl? Her name is, uh... Elena, right?"

Laconically, I nod, trying not to liquefy completely. *Oh. Damn. Fuck.* I can't believe what I'm seeing. No, no, this can't be happening! How many chances did I have for this to happen, huh?

The moment he looks at me, I can tell he's as embarrassed as I am.

"Uh... nice to meet you, I..."

He stands up to shake my hand.

"...My name is Matthew. Matthew Anderson."

I stretch out a shy smile. VERY shy. And most of all: nervous. Why did this asshole lie about his name? Oh, hell... he didn't lie, but he's using his last name on Tinder instead of his first and everyone in the company calls him Matthew. At this level, it's not bad luck, it's breaking a mirror under a ladder in front of a black cat. How am I going to get out of this one?

I can still see myself, a few moments earlier, recounting the juicy details of my one-night stand to Kate. I can't go around with the reputation of the chick who sleeps with her superior, that's not at all the image of myself I want to project. Oh, God... I'm in trouble and no one can help me.

DO NOT TALK ABOUT IT!

"Everything all right, Elena?" asks Betty.

"Y-yes. It's... I'm... I'm fine."

"All right, then. Matt', I want to see you in my office afterwards. I've given you both an assignment. The file is in Elena's hands. Don't let me down."

"Of course," I nod like a good girl.

I stand there for a moment with my arms flailing, and Betty looks at me with her eyebrows furrowed.

"You can go and finish your break if you like."

As I leave the office, Mrs. McGee hot on my heels, I feel as if the whole world has just opened up beneath my feet. It's not a tragedy, it's much worse than that. It's... it's hell! I'm still stunned. My legs feel like they weigh a ton and I'm not even listening to Betty, who's talking to me. I don't care what she says. All I know is that I love books, that I need this job and that this damn one-night stand might cost me. Cost me a lot, in fact.

I try to concentrate on the task at hand, but my thoughts keep returning to Anderson. Well, Matthew. What the hell, whatever his name is! How can I work with him after what happened? I absolutely have to keep this to myself, keep it professional, but how can I ignore this tension between us? I could see it in his eyes. He was embarrassed and at the same time, he gave me half a sneer. Is he amused by all this?

I'm pacing up and down the corridor. I've got about fifteen minutes of break left and I don't know how to use them.

Damn it, damn it, damn it... I slept with my superior!

I take a deep breath and decide to face the situation. I'm going to invest myself in this literary event, prove my professional worth and, hopefully, relegate this night with Matthew to the status of a mere anecdote.

I take a look at the file Betty gave me. OK, it's nothing really: just an open evening at the bookstore, with a few authors. Basically, a nocturne. There's supposed to be a buffet and, of course, she wants the event to be well attended. So, I guess it's going to be a book event. A sort of themed evening.

With this resolution, I head for Matthew's office, determined to discuss the project as if nothing had happened, as if we were simply two colleagues working together. It's my career at stake, and I'm not going to let a one-night stand get in the way.

Entering the room, I find Matthew standing, looking out of the window, his back to me. He turns at my entrance and in his eyes, I read instant surprise, but he tries to compose himself, more professional.

"Elena," he says, regaining his composure and clearing his throat. So, uh... did you... did you look at the file for the event?"

His voice is calm, detached, as if there's nothing between us but work. I reassure myself that it's probably for the best.

"Yes, I've looked through it. There are some interesting ideas, and I think we can really create something unique," I retort, trying to concentrate solely on the project.

Damn, his eyes.

Matthew sits down and invites me to do the same. We start discussing the various aspects of the event, from guest authors to planned activities. I place the folder on his desk and he reaches for it. As he does so, he unintentionally touches my hand, and a wave of electricity runs through me.

God, he has such an effect on me...

Yet there's always this underlying tension, like a big cloud in the room that we both choose to ignore. Every time our eyes meet, there's a spark, a silent reminder of last night.

Stop, Elena, don't think about it! Shit, it's your boss...

"As for promoting the event, I think we should use social networks and maybe organize a few interviews," suggests
Matthew, bringing my attention back to the meeting.

"That's a good idea," I agree. "And maybe a Q&A session
with some of the authors to make them more accessible to
readers."

Who am I trying to look like here? Betty? I'm being ul-
tra-professional when all I really want to do is run away.

The rest of the meeting is a mixture of professional efficien-
cy and personal discomfort. When we finish, Matthew rises to
accompany me out.

"Good work, Elena. I'm sure the event will be a success."

"Thank you, Mr. Anderson. See you tomorrow for further
preparations."

"You... you can call me Matthew."

"Or Mustang?"

Elena! What a bitch...

He moistens his lips and swallows loudly. That's it, I've put
my foot in it and I'm far from ready for it. Without even waiting for his reply, I leave his office and feel his gaze on me. But
I don't look back. I promise myself to keep things strictly professional, no matter how difficult it may be. After all, my career
at the bookstore and my self-respect are at stake.

What the hell is going on?

I think I'm going to faint.

Before going back to work, I go to the bathroom to look at
myself in the mirror. I'm as white as a sheet.

Kate's voice immediately jolts me out of my reverie.

"How are you?"

I turn abruptly, my heart beating a hundred miles an hour.

"Yes, yes, I'm fine. Why wouldn't I be, right?"

Too much haste in my voice. You can tell I'm nervous.

From the way she's looking at me, she knows something's wrong, and I don't want her to go into it. I'm capable of dropping the subject without meaning to. I'm going to sew my mouth shut.

"Okay... I'm going to pretend you're not super weird," she says, washing her hands. "So, how did it go with Betty?"

"Oh, well, er... she's given me an event. I'll have to get on with Anders... well, with Matthew."

"Have you met him?"

Rather, yes, and in detail I've even shared with her, but she can't know that yet. I can't let her know the truth!

Kate may be my best friend, but she's also - and above all - a blabbermouth of the first order, and when I saw the way they were meddling in my private life with Travis....

If they know about this somehow, I think they'll be teasing me until the end of time. But, more importantly, something they said the other day hasn't left my mind: Betty and Matthew are no longer together. And she's the big boss! This is bad. Very, very bad.

What if she still has feelings for him? I mean, really, who works with their ex? That's crazy! Nobody normally does that. It's a shot in the arm to the power of a thousand, and yet it doesn't seem to bother her all that much.

Brr... She was really chilling...

Since I didn't answer Kate's question, she snaps her fingers in front of my eyes, as if trying to wake me up.

"Hey, oh! Earth here! Have you met Matthew?"

"Ah? Er... yes. He's really not attractive..."

My friend is pulling a funny face. It's funny, but I feel like the harder I try to get out, the deeper I sink. It's as if I'm struggling in quicksand.

"Not... attractive?"

"Professionally speaking, I mean. And nothing else."

"You think so? And yet, I assure you he's the best in his field. He's really excellent. You're weird today, aren't you?"

"Not at all. I'll leave you to it."

I take off, leaving Kate at my back.

5

Matthew

It must be a nightmare. I don't see it any other way. No matter how hard I tried to work with her, in the end, I just wanted her to leave. She can't stay here. It's too complicated. On the other hand, I can't fire her either. For one thing, it's not in my remit, and for another, it would be even more suspicious.

It's the one-night stand that could cost me the most of my life...

With Betty... it could get really complicated.

*Will you come and see me in my office?

Talking about the Devil...

Annoyed, I get up to join her. And when I enter, I get a distressed pout. I don't want to see her again. I don't want to talk to her. Every time Betty lays eyes on me and seems to feign this air of infantilizing benevolence, it makes me feel very bad about myself.

"Madam Director," I say.

"Oh, no, please. Please don't start."

"What do you want?"

She clenches her fists.

"Matthew!"

At least she's not accompanied by her brother this time. That's already good news. He's a dickhead, too. I can't even stand him in a painting. The kind of preppy guy who plays golf on Sundays before going to the club for a drink. In short, not at all my kind of guy to hang out with. I can't say I've ever gotten along with my 'brother-in-law'.

Betty tries to pull herself together. I feel she's trying to regain control of her own emotions to appear icier than ever.

Now I recognize my favorite control freak!

Great...

"Have you thought about it?" she asks calmly.

"Yes. And no."

Again, she shows signs of annoyance and frustration, but I don't care.

"We're no longer together. That's all there is to it. I won't change."

Betty shakes her perfect blonde hair and tries to regain some composure.

"You're seeing someone else, aren't you?"

To say the least. I've banged a hell of a lot of women since we broke up. But she hasn't been left out either. If she thinks I don't know what she's playing at...

Betty stares at me, searching my face for an answer to her question. I keep my expression neutral, not wanting to give her the opportunity to probe deeper.

"What I do with my private life is none of your business, Betty," I reply firmly.

She purses her lips, clearly frustrated.

"Matthew, we were good together. You can't deny that..."

I interrupt him, not wanting to let this conversation drag on.

"That's all in the past. Now I'm concentrating on my work

60

and my personal well-being. We should both do the same."

Betty leans back against her desk, her posture conveying a mixture of disappointment and resignation.

"We loved each other, Matthew. So, what happened?"

She gazes at me like a queen with a heart of ice. Her pupils show no emotion whatsoever. Her words say something, but her gaze betrays the opposite. Betty is one of those people who doesn't like. She controls. That's all she is.

"You wanted to control my clothes, Betty. You call that love?"

She squints, as if I'm talking nonsense.

"Of course I did. I was worried about your image, and..."

"Yours. Especially yours. You didn't want to be seen with a guy like me."

She crosses her arms over her chest. When she's like that, I know very well that the next remark is bound to be an assassination.

"But how old are you, Matthew? Maybe it's time to grow up."

"You know very well it's not about that."

"All right, then. If that's your decision... But remember, I'm always here for you if you ever change your mind."

I shake my head slightly, knowing that won't happen.

As I leave her office, I feel a weight lift from my shoulders. The clarity of my decision frees me from the hold she had on me. At least... for now. Every time she tries, I feel like I'm getting more and more stuck. Her words are poison.

But as I walk to my office, thoughts of Elena come back to haunt me. This situation with her could prove disastrous. I have to be careful not to let our brief affair affect our professional collaboration. I can't afford to let my personal life get tangled up with my work, especially not with Betty around.

Arriving at my office, I take a moment to gather my thoughts. I need to stay focused, handle this literary event with Elena as professionally as possible and keep the rest to myself. It's the only way to navigate this complicated situation without causing more damage.

I absolutely must talk to him.

Mid-afternoon, I intercept Kate to ask where Elena is.

"In the storeroom, Matt. Why?"

"We have to organize an event together. I'm going to entrust her with certain tasks."

The bookstore's storeroom is both cluttered and organized. High shelves line the walls, filled with boxes and stacks of unclassified books. Between the shelves, narrow paths lead to different parts of the room, like alcoves cluttered with various things. The lights are dimmed, giving the space an intimate, studious atmosphere. It's into this atmosphere that I stroll to find Elena.

She is currently sorting out the next releases and putting them away with application.

There's something irresistibly appealing about the way she's immersed in her task. Her passion for books and her seriousness, which translates here at work, reminds me why I was captivated by her from the start. From the first Tinder message, I already knew I was attracted to her.

However, recognizing her appeal makes me uncomfortable, given our complex situation. I remind myself that it's essential to maintain a clear boundary between us.

I clear my throat to alert her to my presence.

I'm not about receiving a complaint about harassment in the workplace, either...

"Ah! You startled me, Mr. Anderson."

"Let's stop it, okay?"

"What... what are you talking about?"

I approach her and see that she blushes visibly, then finally lets go of the pile of books she's been holding tightly.

"The formalities, the gentleman and all that. Save it for the business side."

Elena frowns, then shakes her head, trying to look dignified - which suits her quite well, by the way.

"I'm on duty, Mustang. So, what do you want?"

"Listen to me, Woodstock: I don't want anyone to know about this."

No need to specify what.

"Because you think I do?"

Inside, I'm bubbling over. What do I know?

"I don't know you and I don't know what you're capable of."

Woodstock looks at me, outraged.

Now's the time to resist making out with him in the storeroom, out of sight.

I feel this magnetic attraction between us. I'm a magnet, and she's a piece of metal. But I have to stand my ground. If I give in now, it's over. Even more than it already is. And I won't be able to resist my own desires for long. The only solution is for her to leave.

It can't be any other way. I could never work with her. And Betty has the good idea of putting us on the same event... As if I needed that.

"Do you really think I want to tell everyone I slept with my superior? Are you crazy, Mustang? I don't want to look like the service whore in the bookstore."

"Good. Perfect. We have common interests, then."

But you're still going to have to leave, Woodstock, I'm sorry...

"On the other hand," I continue, "you won't last long here."

I use my driest, most authoritative voice possible. Fuck, I like her and I can't tell her.

"What is it? Why?"

"Look at this work," I say, pointing to the books she's just put away. "Start all over again. It's all nonsense."

"Huh? But I..."

"Start over," I cut her off. "No discussion."

At these words, I turn on my heels to leave the storeroom.

This is just the beginning. In a week at the most, she'll be gone.

6

Elena

Note to self: guys who drive Mustangs are really obnoxious assholes. I thought that with a profile like his, he'd be more accommodating, nicer, and not act like the worst kind of asshole. Okay, I had his eyes in my head all evening - and even most of the night - but now I just want to rip them out. Start all over again? And in the name of what? I'm sure it's a job well done. He's just messing with me. But if he wants war, he'll get it. I've read enough books and genres to have ideas to defend myself. I'm not going to be pushed around that easily. If he wants to abuse his position, I can play too. Not in the same way, not with the same weapons, but just as effectively.

In the break room, on the stroke of 4 p.m., Kate tells me:

"So, what's on tap for tonight?"

"Reading evening."

At the same time, Matthew enters the room for a coffee.

"Yeah, yeah, 'reading' evening," she continues, "sketching hooks with her fingers. I know someone who's going to see her beautiful stallion from the other night!"

Couldn't she just shut the hell up? Matthew turns in our direction, then arches an eyebrow, before returning to his coffee.

Shit, shit, shit.

"Stop it, Kate. You can't say that."

"Don't be such a prude. Matthew doesn't care if you're worried. He doesn't even listen to what we say. Travis and I talk about sex in front of him all the time and he doesn't react."

I'm not so sure about that. Right now, he looks pretty attentive.

"Yeah, but..."

"Come on, I'm sure you'll get caught like a goddess in his car again. Aren't you?"

This time, I even notice a discreet smile on Matthew's face. I don't know where to put myself anymore. Definitely, I want to liquefy myself and go under the linoleum, never to come out again.

"Stop it! No, I swear I'm only going to read. Will you stop talking about this date right now?"

"Oh, but it seems to bother her, too, the naughty girl! You weren't this shy when you were riding him until you broke your coccyx."

It is. Worse. Worse. And. Worse.

Every word Kate says is like another nail in my coffin. It's horrible. She doesn't dose at all on the details, which she shrugs off without shaking a knee. I feel like I'm going to faint. If she keeps this up, I swear I'm going to send her a phalanx so powerful she won't be hungry for years.

"Stop, stop, stop..."

Oh, boy, I don't know where to put myself. I think I'll go and bury myself in a corner, or under a piece of furniture, and die there like an old cat. In the meantime, to dodge this MORE THAN EMBARRASSING conversation, I decide to go back to work. I don't mind cutting into my break. I have no desire to be in the same room as Kate, at the same time as Matthew. Not for the world.

I've got a mountain of labeling to do anyway. That's good. I'll be able to forget Matthew's big eyes for a few more hours and then I'll go home and get under the comforter to read -

and *really* read! I think that's the best option.

I head for the storeroom, grabbing a pile of books waiting to be labeled and filed. Manual work is a blessing: it allows me to concentrate on something tangible and concrete, far removed from emotional complications.

I can't believe this is happening to me...

Fortunately, this job is fun. Each book I pick up is a little world in itself, an escape, and I lose myself in the titles, authors and genres. It's soothing and, in a way, therapeutic. I feel calmer, more grounded, as I line up the books on the shelves, finding a place for them all.

The late afternoon passes, slowly but surely. The shadows lengthen in the reserve, and the calm of the place is only disturbed by the occasional sound of my movements. It's a welcome solitude, a moment for myself, away from the day's complications.

When my work is finally done, I take one last satisfied look at the perfectly organized storeroom. It's time to go home, slip under my comforter and lose myself in a good book. Just me, my thoughts, and the words dancing before my eyes. I'll finish tomorrow. It's absolutely impossible to finish all this today. Apparently, we've just received some big packages and we've got all week to finish it.

As I leave the reserve, I come face to face with Matthew. This time, he doesn't seem at all pleased to see me. Quite the opposite, in fact. It's as if he's angry, even.

"Where are you going?"

"Well, I'm... going home. I'm done for the night, and..."

Without giving me time to finish, he raises his hand in front of me, telling me to be quiet.

What's gotten into him all of a sudden?

He passes his eyes over my work, then plants his gaze in mine.

"Feel like you're done here?"

"No, I haven't finished, but it's already 7p.m. and the bookstore is closed, so..."

"The bookstore, perhaps, but not the offices."

I frown. I don't see what he's getting at.

"What do you want, Mustang?"

"Don't call me that. Is that clear?"

He doesn't look at all like the friendly, laughing guy I met the other night. He's turning into a super-henchman, if I'm not mistaken.

"What's been going on with you since I arrived? Are you afraid for your job?"

Matthew gets carried away and frames me between his arms, against a shelf. From where I stand, I can smell his woody scent and the warmth of his breath. Inside him, I can tell by the color of his eyes, he's up a storm.

"Listen to me, Woodstock..."

"I thought we weren't supposed to call each other by nickname..."

"I don't even remember your name, and I don't need to remember it, because I don't want you to stay in this box. Is that clear?"

He tells me this outright. Without a hair out of place, he stares into my eyes like a stake.

"I intend to make my mark here. I've always dreamed of working in a bookstore. You can't take that away from me."

He smiles slightly, then takes a step back.

"No. That's true. But I can ask you to continue with the labeling because it's not finished yet."

My eyes go wide. Is he kidding me? It's not possible and he knows it. I'll be here... all night. And even part of the morning!

"What? But..."

"Is that a problem?"

Of course it is! What does he think?

"You have no right to..."

"To what? Asking you to work? I think so. Labeling was on your to-do list today. I checked the schedule. If you can't keep up, you'd better stay home."

I see how he plays it.

He goes from being a nice guy to a completely tyrannical boss. But if he thinks he's got me, he's got the wrong guy.

"You know something? Nobody's waiting for me at home. So, I don't care," I reply dryly, getting back to work.

"You shouldn't be proud of it. It's pretty pathetic."

"You know you're a real bastard?"

Matthew frowns, and I can't help but be irresistibly drawn to the look of annoyance on his face. Why should that be? It should be the other way around. Is it because of her Apollo body, which I can see beneath her clothes? I've already taken advantage of his muscles and I have to admit they attract me. Every time he looks at me, I have the strange feeling that he's undressing me.

I have a feeling that working here is going to be more than difficult...

"I don't really care. Finish this by tomorrow, Woodstock. This better be over by the time I get back."

He turns on his heels, proud of his last reply, both scathing and unpleasant.

"Or else what?" I shout behind his back.

Matthew glances over his shoulder at me, sparkling and angry at the same time. His tone is unchallenging, yet I insist.

"I'm going to have to crack down."

Are we still talking about work here? I feel like we're drifting...

"Really? Is that so? By taking your subordinate in your car, for example, and spanking her?"

He clenches his jaw. I've just reminded him of a memory I think he'd rather forget.

"No. By giving you a warning."

The bastard.

This time, he turns on his heel for good and slams the door behind him, leaving me alone in the storeroom with my tags. And so it goes. The charming 'Anderson' is going to turn into a real tyrannical prick. I don't think I'm going to enjoy this game at all.

The night is long, interminable. Every book I label seems to weigh down my eyelids more and more. I work methodically, but with overwhelming slowness. The hours pass, and fatigue accumulates in every muscle of my body. The storeroom becomes my world, a world of silence and solitude, interrupted only by the rustle of pages and the clatter of my machine.

I don't even have time to think about Matthew anymore. I'm far too busy dying of exhaustion inside. It's just awful.

As the first light of morning begins to filter through the windows, I finally finish the labeling. My eyes burn with fatigue, and my body cries out for rest. I realize that I only have a short time before the employees arrive for another day's work.

I hate him. Seriously, I hate him.

I head for the break room, exhausted. I grab an old cushion and lie down on the uncomfortable sofa. I close my eyes, hoping to glean a few precious minutes of sleep.

Sleep, when it comes, is restless and unrefreshing. Images of Matthew, of our tense exchanges and of our night together, crowd my dreams. I wake with a start several times, my heart beating wildly.

"Hey, oh, groundhog!" says Kate. "What the hell are you doing here?"

My eyes burn so much I feel like I've rubbed them with a piece of lemon. I try to forget, for a few moments, that I'm exhausted, then open my mouth to answer my friend, but almost nothing comes out.

"I... I..."

"Wait, you slept there?"

I guess so.

It's Travis's turn to enter the break room. When he sees me lying on the couch, he raises an eyebrow in surprise.

"Uh... Elena?"

"No comment. For pity's sake," I say.

I'm exhausted. I've just finished working and I've already got to get back to work.

"But why didn't you go home?" says Kate.

"I had to finish labeling the books that had just arrived."

"Books that have just...? But... they don't go on sale until next week," says Kate. "Why did you start so early?"

What a bastard. No, really, what a bastard! I get it. He's doing everything he can to get me to leave. But it won't work. I'm going to resist him so much that he's going to be the one to let go. I'm not usually a girl who looks for trouble. Far from it. In fact, I'm more the conciliatory type. I try to understand everyone's opinion so I can form my own, and I take other people's sensitivities into account before I say or do anything. But once these barriers are crossed, I become a bull ready to charge. To put it more simply: I'm nice, but you can't look for me too much either. Otherwise, I'll be found. And right now, Matthew has clearly broken one of the barriers. I can't let him push me around like this. His behavior is simply intolerable.

"I just... I wanted to get a head start, that's all."

For the time being, I'll keep a low profile. No need to alert everyone with these stories. I'll talk directly to Matthew. Eye to eye. We need to sort this out between us before it rubs off any further on our professional relationship.

The worst part is that I haven't finished...

"Well, I've got to get back to it," I say. "Matthew's not here yet?"

"No," retorts Travis. "Not for another hour, I think."

I intend to have it over before he arrives. I refuse to have failed.

I return to the storeroom, determined to finish what I've started.

7

Matthew

Okay, I've been a jerk, but I'm not going to apologize for it. Elena has to go. There's no other way. When I get to the bookstore, I wonder how I'm going to give her a hard time. I imagine she hasn't finished what I ordered her to do. I don't think that's possible. Humanly speaking, I mean. She wouldn't have had all night to finish labeling all the books, so I'm not too worried about that.

If Betty finds out that the new employee she just hired was my one-night stand... We're both dead.

Elena has no idea how much trouble we're in. It has to be said that Betty isn't the type to play around. Especially when it comes to me. She'd put us both through hell. So, cruel as it is, I have to face the facts: it's either Elena or me. And as far as possible, I'd like her to be the one to get out. I've almost reached the end of my dream by reupholstering my van, I'm not about to give it up so easily because of a stupid hook-up on Tinder. When I'm done, I'm going to get the hell out of here, drive around the coast and surf to my heart's content. If Elena becomes an obstacle in my path, then I'll have to treat her like one.

I push open the storeroom door and look for her between the shelves, before finding her asleep, a book in her hand.

She'll hear me.

"Get up! What the hell are you doing? Were you sleeping?"

"Huh? I..."

"What are you going to say for yourself, huh?"

At first, her face is flushed with surprise, which gradually turns to cold anger.

"That it wasn't possible and you knew it! Besides, these books are on sale for next week. I've been informed, believe me. I'm not going to give in that easily."

She's resilient, too. Looks like she won't be an easy kill. Far from it. I underestimated Elena, character-wise. She seems to have some after all. It's not going to make my job any easier, but I'm not going to give up just yet.

Her eyebrows are furrowed and there are dark circles under her eyes. But I don't think she cares. I'm not even listening to her, even though she's blaming me.

She's so sexy when she gets angry like that...

"Do you think it's right to ask a subordinate to do that? No, Mustang. Yeah, I did call you Mustang, so you'd remember what happened the other night. Although, in view of your behavior, I have to say that I'd rather forget. You used to be a really nice guy, and now you've turned into the world's biggest asshole!"

"Quiet. Not so loud. If I asked you to label these books, it's because Betty asked me to."

Elena crosses her arms over her chest, then looks at me sternly.

"Ah, yes, I see. You've given me your job."

She's a quick study, I see.

I shrug my shoulders to get rid of the problem, but she steps into the breach.

"So, if I go and tell Betty, she's going to square you up, is she?"

Just the thought of it sends a chill down my spine. Woodstock doesn't realize how difficult my situation is. If I'm in a bad mood with Betty, it weakens me in her eyes, and I can't afford that. I have to remain totally professional and beyond reproach. Otherwise, she might try to manipulate me by mixing the professional and the private, as she used to do. In the past, this could take the form of various forms of advantage, and today I don't feel like owing her anything. Not the slightest favor. I want to be perfectly free to do what I want without needing Betty's support, or her having me on her radar.

"Don't get on my nerves, Woodstock, this really isn't the time."

"Oh, sorry, did 'monsieur' sleep badly? Because I did, you see. I've got 1 hour of sleep behind me, give or take, which I spent in the break room. Then, I was so exhausted that I fell asleep here while doing YOUR work. So, if you don't mind, I'd like to have a little chat with management. I think two minutes will be enough.

All right, fine. I screwed up. She's got me.

Instead of letting her escape, I block her path, then pick up a book to label it in turn.

"So, you're getting your hands dirty now?" she remarks suspiciously.

"Don't mess with me either, okay? I'm doing this as a courtesy. If you think Betty's going to listen to you any more than I do, you're up to your elbows in it. I'm just trying to keep us out of trouble. You and me both. So just take these books and label them. There's half of them left. If the two of us work together, we should finish quickly."

She sighs, rubs her eyes, then nods as she continues her meticulous work.

I shouldn't be with her, or at least not that close physically. For some reason I can't explain, Elena attracts me. It's as if her whole being is calling to me. Except I don't feel like giving in. Not like this. It would cause us even more trouble and yet, I'm not a fool: I see the looks she gives me, and, above all, I still have fresh memories of the evening we spent together. And it was magical. It was the best one-night stand I'd ever had. I'd like to do it again, that's clear, but now's not the time.

And it never will be.

"So, you and Betty..."

"I don't want to talk about that at all."

"We've got to keep busy, don't we?" she protests.

"Less blah and more labeling. It's not like you're the queen of speed, in that respect."

She drops the book in her hands, then gives me a look full of lightning.

"You're not? Maybe you're not the king of ideal sons-in-law either. To think that I thought about you the day after... I'm so sorry."

Did she? Did she do that?

Because so have I.

"You shouldn't have attached so much importance to it. That's your problem, Woodstock, not mine."

There was a real connection.

"I had the feeling there was more," she continues.

"You made a mistake. You're imagining things."

"Really, it's not tact that's suffocating you."

"If you keep talking..."

"What's the matter? Are you going to shut me up?"

Is this some kind of challenge? Because, if so...

"Just so you know, I could do it without too much trouble."

I don't like it at all when she challenges me like that. She doesn't know what I'm capable of.

"What are you waiting for?" she asks.

The cheeky one.

"You shouldn't be playing this game with me. Believe me, you could regret it."

Damn, she tempts me.

She always has this angry look on her face, like she's going to explode at any moment, and instead of feeling upset, I melt. I hate being like this. I don't want to be at the mercy of her charm when I'm supposed to be her superior. I don't want us to have a relationship when... it would make things even more complicated. I won't do it.

"There's nothing you can do," she asserts confidently.

"You don't know what you're talking about."

" So come on, Mustang, show me."

This is too much. I grab Elena by the hips and pin her against one of the bookcases. Our eyes meet in a growing electricity. I feel our eyes flash and the air becomes charged with an almost palpable tension. I won't be able to resist my urges for long if she keeps teasing me. Every time she calls me Mustang, I'm reminded of the evening we spent together and a part of me - below the belt - longs to do it again.

"Do you have a book to label in your pocket, or are you just very happy to see me?" she murmurs.

I hate her.

She gets me out of my funk. Normally, I'm a self-controlled guy. I have full control of my body and mind. But in her presence, it's as if all my circuits are wavering and I'm unresponsive. I've tried to keep my distance from her, but it's just not possible. We work in the same bookstore and have to put on an event together. Betty has no idea how much she's going to test my nerves by forcing me to collaborate with Elena.

"Stop teasing me..." I hiss through my teeth.

"Or else what?"

My eyes are fixed on his lips. We're drawn to each other; with a power I struggle to realize. To ask why would be completely pointless. It's almost... animal.

"I'll shut you up."

"Go ahead."

Without warning, I glue my lips to hers in an ardent bestiality. It's both electric and... impulsive. Elena lets herself go, as if delighted to be at my mercy.

Fuck, we're in the bookstore... I shouldn't... I so shouldn't!...

But I can't help it. My mouth explores hers with unparalleled greed. And Elena is not to be outdone in her urges either. I see they're shared. So, I'm not crazy. This connection, this attraction I feel for her: it's mutual. And I revel in it. Every time her hand grazes my skin, it's a whirlwind of sensations.

But to keep her from charming me even more, I hold her against the bookcase.

"Is that all you've got?"

She continues to play the strong head even though she's out of breath.

"You were sharper in the car, Woodstock."

"Do you really want me to show you what I can do?"

As she slips her hand into my pants, I do the same, slipping the elastic of her panties, and we both begin a kind of implicit challenge. Who will make the other come first?

Really, I shouldn't...

But never mind. Now that it's started, I don't really care how it ends. Besides, it's no longer just a matter of torrid foreplay between her and me, during which our hands explore the most intimate parts of our bodies. No. It's now a duel. I don't see it as anything other than a confrontation.

The others will be here soon. Damn it, we've got to stop here before things get out of hand.

My fingers slide inside her, and I begin to search her, sinking deeper and deeper. My thumb is already circling her swollen clit. For her part, she's taken hold of my stiff cock and is shamelessly jerking me off.

Damn. She's good.

"Is that all, Mustang?" she gasps.

"If you have condoms, we can go further. But I don't suppose you walk around with them?"

"I'm ready for anything."

"That's going too far."

"Too far for you?"

And she continues to defy me.

But I've got it under control. I know what to do, and soon Elena is no longer able to stifle her moans of pleasure. She finally releases her grip and clings to the furniture, panting.

"Getting cold feet, Woodstock? I think you're starting to lose your footing."

"Shut... up..."

We make a mad scramble. Books tip over, shelves shake and the echo of our voices echoes against the bookstore walls. Early in the morning, it's amazing how much fun you can have.

"Matthew... I'm... I'm gonna come, I..."

The moment I feel her contract around me, I decide to pull back sharply, to read all the frustration in her eyes. I place my hand authoritatively on her sex.

"What the...?"

"Don't ever upset me again."

Once again, my fingers slip into her pleasure-dampened intimacy and get busy. She nods, breathless, but I come out again.

"Do you understand?" I ask, rubbing her bud with my fingertips for the pleasure of watching her squirm.

"Either fuck me or give up. But don't beat around the bush."

"Are you the pot?"

"Shut your mouth. You're an annoying guy. You know that?"

"I get that a lot, you know," I retort, withdrawing for good.

I remove my hand from her panties and challenge her with my eyes. This time, I've definitely won, and I can tell by the reproachful expression on her face.

"Are you really going to stop there?"

At the same time, I hear a door close to the storeroom being opened and someone approaching.

Crap.

8

Elena

I'm frustrated and have a furious urge to punch Matthew in the face. Especially after what he just did to me. No, seriously, what a bastard. Pushing me to the breaking point and refusing to give me the orgasm I deserve. When it comes to bastards, he's at the top of the list.

Someone approaches us, cutting short our exchange.

I must not compromise myself with him.

I don't want to be seen as the kind of girl who sleeps with her superior. That's not what I want at all, and it's not the image I want to project of myself. I'm better than that. I won't let him convince me otherwise.

Matthew is really annoying. But then, when he runs his hand through his hair - the other one, not the one he used to, um... well... there you go - he looks more than cute. And then, the smile he gives me: it's worth all the warnings in the world about what could happen again in this bookstore. That says a lot about his intentions. The more I get to know him, the less I understand him. There's this fickleness about him that I don't like at all. One minute he's blowing hot, the next he's blowing cold. It's as if there's no in between.

"Shit, you're REALLY going to stop there, then," I grumble between my teeth.

81

"Shhh. No one must know that..."

"What? That we were making out in the storeroom? No kidding?" I murmur as I hear footsteps approaching.

I can't believe I dared to do such a thing myself. I'm pretty used to unexpected events in the stories I read, and I love them, but surely not in *real life*! Matthew is real. And the thing about annoying guys like him is that they're only cute in romantic comedies. In reality, you just want to slap them in the face because they refuse to make you come...

"Shut up..." he threatens me in a low voice.

I quickly readjust my clothes before the door opens. It's Ray McGee, crossing the threshold into the storeroom.

I didn't really get a chance to talk to him when I bumped into him in the big boss's office. I don't even really know what his role is in the bookstore. All I know is that most of the time, he's in the management offices and doesn't leave. Kate and Travis have very little gossip about him, so they make up crazy rumors. But hey, I don't believe a word of it.

I notice that he is always very well groomed. Which is, in my opinion, a bit creepy. His blond hair plastered back with half a ton of gel, he sets his piercing eyes on us. They're the same as Betty's.

"Hey, Ray, what the hell are you doing here?" asks Matthew with a faux casual air.

"I heard a noise. I wondered if everything was all right."

Matthew shrugs, then gives me a look. I realize I must imitate him. I play along and shrug my shoulders.

"Yeah, all's well," he retorts. "And you, still burnt out on self-tanner?"

Ray's only response is to give him a monumental middle finger, before turning on his heels. Wow, that's what I call a nice show of respect.

"It was a close call," says Mustang, turning to me.

"It's all your fault. Besides, you didn't finish what you started and I blame you, a lot."

"Is that so? Well, that makes two of us," Matthew teases me,
pointing to the books that haven't been labeled yet.

Oh, I see, what a bastard. He really has no intention of finishing!

"Anyway," I continue, "it won't happen again. Everything
that happened here was an unfortunate accident.

"I agree with that. I don't intend to let it happen again. It's
gone too far."

Hey! I thought he'd react! Not that he'd confirm.

All this puts us in an extremely delicate situation. I'm torn
between a hard-to-control attraction and a hell of a lot of re-
sentment towards him.

"What's this guy's role here?" I ask, trying to take my mind
off things.

"Think of Ray as a sort of demonic sorcerer."

"From... eh?"

"Yeah, a guy who manipulates demons," he retorts, labeling
a new book.

I frown.

"And... why?"

"He's a salesman. What else would he be? Besides, he's always with Betty. He's her brother."

Ah, hence the similar creepy look. OK, now I understand...

"Matthew?" asks a female voice as she enters the storeroom.

When we talk about the she-wolf, we see her tail...

Oops. I'm feeling increasingly uncomfortable. Everyone is
trickling into the bookstore and they obviously already know
that Mustang and I are squatting in the storeroom.

If she knew what just happened here...

"Matt, I need to talk to you. I need to talk to you now."

She doesn't even bother to say hello. It's as if I don't exist.

Well, I have a feeling that in addition to being a shadowy little hand, I have another superpower: invisibility.

Matthew gives me an annoyed look, sighs, then follows his boss for that famous conversation that seems to really - *really* - delight him. It doesn't concern me. But a second after he leaves the room, I realize he's also taken the labeler with him. Oh, hell no...

I need coffee. And the labeler!

Determined to finish my work, I decide to find Matthew. He can't be far away...

I thread my way through the bookstore's shelves, guided by Betty's voice, which echoes between two shelves. Even though she's trying to tone it down and make it as unobtrusive as possible, I can hear from her inflections that she's annoyed. At least, too much to contain.

"Matthew, I'm serious. You can't just throw away everything we've built together overnight. There's still a chance we can make it work. My parents think we're still together, but they haven't seen you in a while and they're starting to wonder. You've got to come home."

I shouldn't be here, listening. I so shouldn't. Yet the urge to listen is irresistible. And I'm so curious that I can't take my ears off what I'm hearing.

"Oh, let me guess: they don't like to know that their beloved daughter is single? It's not very glamorous, is it? Does it tarnish your image as a businesswoman?"

Betty's voice goes up a notch, betraying her frustration.

"It's not about image, Matthew! It's about... what we had together. It's important to me, you know?"

I approach discreetly, trying to stay out of sight. Matthew answers, his voice low and controlled:

"Betty, it's over. There's nothing to save. I've moved on."

There's a pause, a silence heavy with tension. Then Betty

resumes, her voice trembling slightly.

"Is there anyone else?"

I hold my breath.

Will he talk about me? Will he reveal our secret?

"No, it's not that," Matthew replies. "It's just that... I need to think about myself, about what's right for me. And being with you isn't what's right for me anymore."

I feel a pang of relief. He doesn't mention anything about our night together. It's a secret between us.

Betty seems about to retort but stops herself. She sighs.

"This situation is untenable, and you know it."

"For whom?" he hisses. "Because I can live with that."

I can't hear the polar blonde anymore, yet I can feel her rage. It's as if all her anger is palpable and spreading through the bookstore like wildfire. She hates having this conversation - and how I understand her. It can't be pleasant at all. Especially since Matthew is so firm. I wonder what could have happened between them for him to be so adamant.

"Five years. You want to throw it all away?"

"Yes."

"You know I can just as easily fire you. I can't have you hanging around here anymore."

"So go ahead. What are you waiting for?"

Mmh... she can't take it anymore, but on the other hand, this situation must be good for her too. Whatever happens, she keeps a certain control over him through this job. They're in a complex situation, both of them.

Betty takes a deep breath, as if gathering her thoughts.

"I'm not going to fire you, Matthew. That would be too easy. But I can't go on seeing you every day, pretending nothing's happened."

There's a harshness in her voice that betrays her inner struggle. Matthew, for his part, remains stoic, almost impassive.

"So, what do you suggest?" he asks.

"A change of department. You won't be under my direct responsibility anymore. You'll be working on another project, away from me."

I sense that Matthew is about to protest.

"Are you taking the piss? No, I've still got some unfinished business at my post."

"You might as well work with Ray."

"Your stupid brother? I hate him. He's as dumb as a rock, and even then, his toes probably have more conversation than he does.

Betty is furious.

"I forbid you to... rah... You put me through hell. Do you know that?"

"Don't worry," he retorts dryly. "In a little while, I'll be gone."

Once again, she sighs.

"Chasing your stupid dream, right?"

There's a moment's silence.

"Don't you think there's more to it than that? How old are you, Matthew?" adds Betty, as if to prick him.

"There's no age for dreams. Just because you don't have any doesn't mean you should begrudge others theirs."

That's where I agree with Matthew. You must never give up.

"Especially if you're going away with your mates! That's really stupid. They're dragging you down, you know?"

"Ah, because you don't?" he sneers.

Betty seems to be gritting her teeth.

"I offered you a situation."

"Which I didn't want," retorts Matthew.

"You're an ungrateful bastard. Do you remember everything you learned, thanks to me?"

Matthew bursts out laughing.

"Oh, yes: giving up everything you love to make yourself look good. A great philosophy of life, Betty. Thanks a lot, Betty. Don't wait up for the next family barbecue, okay? I'll pass."

Now it's her turn to laugh.

"I see. I'll tell you what. Do whatever you want. After all, you're free, aren't you? But if I find out it's for another girl, I swear..."

Preferably, I wouldn't want to be taken to task in this kind of argument; I don't think any good can come of it, as far as I'm concerned. I'm going to have to make myself very small.

But hey, it's not like there's anything going on between Matthew and me, right?

"Yeah? You'll do what?"

"I'll make her so miserable that the last thing she'll want is to see you again. Or even live. I don't like people messing with my stuff, especially without my consent."

I jump up in spite of myself and shrivel up against the shelf that hides me.

So that's how she sees it? It's a bit... sinister, though. I find this woman really horrible. The more I learn about her, the less I like her.

"I don't belong to you," he squeaks.

"Right. In the meantime, I pay your salary, don't I? And it's thanks to that salary that you can fix up your crappy van. So, keep quiet."

I can hear them walking away, each on their own, the tension between them palpable even from a distance. I stay hidden for a while, digesting what I've heard. This revelation about their past relationship and Betty's decision makes me think about the complexity of human relationships, especially in a professional environment. I'd never worked in a big company before. When Kate sold me the bookstore, she said: "Don't worry! It's like a big family here!" Yeah, and in a family there's a lot of bickering, unspoken things and implicit hierarchies.

I emerge from my hiding place, my mind muddled. I need to focus on my work, but it's hard to ignore the undertones of this conversation. I wonder how this will affect Matthew, his work and, by extension, mine.

With a sigh, I return to my tasks, promising myself to keep a professional distance from Matthew, despite our recent near-coitus. The situation at the bookstore has just become even more complicated, and I must remain vigilant.

Matthew returns, labeler in hand. He doesn't look happy at all, and I don't feel like telling him everything I've heard.

Together, we get back to labeling, but quite honestly, he doesn't look happy to be there. Which I can understand. I'd like to break the ice between us again, but I don't know how.

After a few minutes of tense silence, I take a deep breath and decide to make the first move.

"Matthew, I just... I wanted to say I'm sorry about before. I shouldn't have provoked you like that."

He pauses for a moment, his eyes fixed on the books in front of him, then looks at me.

"Thank you, Elena. It's just... everything's complicated right now."

"I understand," I answer softly. "And I want you to know that... what happened between us, stays between us."

He nods, visibly relieved.

"I really appreciate this. That's the last thing I need... More complications..."

We get back to work and the atmosphere seems a little lighter. I venture to ask another question, hoping to gain a better understanding of the situation.

"Are you okay with Betty?"

"How do you know I'm having trouble with her?"

Oops. Now I'm stuck. I wanted to push the conversation, but I went too far.

"I... actually, I wanted to get the labeler back, and uh... I overheard... well... I overheard a few snatches of your conversation."

Matthew sighs.

"Yes. I'll be okay. I'll just have to adapt, that's all. I'm used to it. Thanks for your concern."

There is a pause, then he adds:

"You know, Elena, I... I didn't want things to be like this between us. You're a really interesting person and I would have liked to have met you under different circumstances. But this..."

I feel my cheeks redden slightly. I'm touched by his sincere compliment.

"Me too, I would have loved to. But you make do with what you have, right?"

He sketches a sad smile.

"Exactly. We make do with what we have."

The rest of the day is spent in quiet but efficient work. The tension has dissipated somewhat, replaced by a mutual understanding of our complicated situation. I don't know what the future holds, but for now we're content to work side by side, sharing the secret of what happened between us.

I have to stay away from him.

This must never happen again. Never again.

9

Matthew

What a shitty day. It's unbearable to still be working here when I should already be far away. I hate this place. I didn't used to. Now that Betty and I aren't together, staying here has become an ordeal. And what's more, when I step outside, I find it's raining. Great. No fine, cooling droplets. No. A nice big shower.

An end to the day to match the day.

I rev my Mustang's engine, then start it up.

Driving through the city, the rain drums on the roof of the car, punctuating my thoughts. I think of Betty, of our past and how everything has changed. It was a relationship that shaped me in some way but is now a source of pain and regret.

I'm also thinking about Elena, our unspoken tension and the complexity of our relationship. There's something about her that attracts me, but I know I have to keep my distance.

It's too complicated.

I shouldn't be thinking about her. But I can't help it. I can still see her eyes. The passion we both felt when we were together on the reservation and things got so much... hotter. I still want more. I've totally canceled my upcoming dates. Not my style at all. But when I scroll through Tinder, I can't help but think back to her and what we've been through. I've rarely had so much to connect with another person. I think she and I understand each other. It's very strange, because deep down, I hardly know her at all.

As I turn off into a side street, still close to the bookstore, I catch a glimpse of her. She's hiding under her coat, trying to avoid the pouring rain.

Don't stop. Don't stop. Don't stop.

Shit, I don't want to get stuck in the car with her again. It feels like it could get out of hand at any minute. On the other hand, I can't leave her like this.

What the...

I stop at his level and open the window.

"Elena? What are you...? Get in the car!"

She turns to me, but I feel like she's hesitating. Like she's sizing me up.

"What? Would you rather stand in the rain?"

"Are you going to blow hot and cold again? I'm not sure I want to join you."

"Don't be silly. Is it because I'm in the thriller section too?"

She arches an eyebrow. In the rain, all her make-up is running off and she looks even prettier.

"What do you mean?"

"Because I know how to hide a body, or make it disappear. But, I promise, I'm not a serial killer. You'd better get in or you'll freeze to death."

Elena bursts out laughing, and despite the heavy, dark, rain-laden sky, it suddenly feels like the sun is shining on us.

Convinced, she climbs into the Mustang.

"Still a beautiful car," she comments with a smile.

"Thanks. Oh, actually, I take very good care of it."

"By inviting strangers inside?"

Her candid air is both ravishing and irresistible. Why do I think that? I shouldn't let myself be seduced like that. It's almost too easy. It's really getting tiresome. But that's how it is. Elena has something in her eyes that attracts me. A sparkle, a glint, that of a woman who hasn't yet achieved what she set out to do, and who has an inordinate ambition. Maybe that's what attracted me to Betty. The difference was that with my ex, this characteristic could become a toxic trait. *Ambition at all costs.* With Elena, it's very different. I don't feel that. It's as if she's quiet on the inside, but still smoldering, ready to take everything in her path. It's an ambivalence that's hard to describe.

"You're not a stranger anymore."

"Because we made out in the car?"

I laugh.

"If it was just making out… Where do you want a lift?"

"Same place as last time."

I stretch half a smile across my face. It's true that I still know the address. Strangely enough, it's as if it's engraved in me.

"Would you like to make a little detour?"

Elena gives me a puzzled look.

"Where to?"

I shrug and smile.

"One of my favorite places. It's a spot I love and I'd love to show it to you."

"Gosh, decide. Are we co-workers, or does it go a little deeper than that?

"I'm just showing a newcomer the best parts of San Francisco. There's nothing wrong with that, is there?"

Liar.

Why am I stalling like this? Am I really enjoying staying with her? I know I should stay away from her. Not just for my sake, but for hers too. I feel like I'm playing with fire, and I've got to admit: it's kind of fun. Especially when the flame is this hot. Elena is nothing like any other girl. I can see it when my eyes land on her and I catch her tender gaze. She wanders everywhere, as if discovering the city with eyes full of wonder. I want to show her off too.

"Mmh mmh," she retorts. Of course she does. "Do you think I'm stupid? I'm sure you've driven lots of girls around town, only to lay them out in that Mustang."

"Here? Are you delirious? No, I guarantee it was the first time."

"You're a talker."

She makes me laugh. Worst of all, I'm telling the truth.

"It's true, I assure you," I insist. "You are an exception."

Elena shakes her head, a smirk forming on her lips. She doesn't seem totally convinced, but she doesn't protest any further. How can she still be single?

I have to put these thoughts out of my mind. It can't be done.

"So, show me this famous place," she says, settling comfortably into the passenger seat.

I drive through the streets where it's now night, the rain having stopped, leaving behind a damp road that glistens under the city lights. The silence between us is no longer so tense; there's a kind of complicity that's taken root, a subtle game of seduction and denial. I don't want to be the one to make the first move. I cracked earlier. And rather easily. I don't want that to happen again. I think it would end up giving her a bad opinion of me.

After a few minutes, I park on a promontory overlooking the city. The lights of San Francisco twinkle below, offering a magical spectacle.

"Wow, it's... it's beautiful," breathes Elena, admiring the view.

I turn to her, noticing the gleam of wonder in her eyes.

"I like coming here to think. It gives me a different perspective on things."

We stand in silence for a moment, each of us lost in thought, watching the city stretch out at our feet. It's a moment of peace, far removed from the complexity of our daily lives.

Finally, Elena turns to me, her eyes sparkling.

"Thank you for showing me this place. It's... it's a beautiful gift."

"I'm glad you like it."

"Is this where you come to reflect on life?"

We're so close that I can almost feel her breath against mine, and the warmth of her skin, without even touching her.

"Well... yes, a little," I admit. "But we can think about it together. No problem for me."

This seems to satisfy her.

"Well," she suggests, "why don't we start by breaking the ice again?"

"What do you mean by that?"

Elena shrugs.

"I'm Elena. My favorite color is green," she says, holding out her hand.

Instead of taking her seriously, I burst out laughing. But her insistence forces me to play along.

Oh, boy.

"Well, uh... Matthew," I retort, grabbing her hand. "My favorite color is orange. Twilight orange, preferably."

"Very poetic. It's already more in line with what I know about 'Anderson'."

"Who's Anderson?" I feign.

Elena puts a finger against her chin and pretends to think.

"Oh, a creep who pretends to be something he's not, hoping to sleep with women."

"He does that? What a bastard..."

"You're telling me."

"But maybe he has his reasons."

She arches an eyebrow, then smiles.

"Oh yes, and which ones?"

"Maybe... Anderson has a complicated past and has just gone through a break-up that he's having trouble digesting. And then, maybe there's his ex who's bothering him. She could, you know, give him a hard time.

"You seem well informed."

"Yeah. He's a pal," I giggle.

"Anyway, I thought he was really cute," admits Elena.

This remark sends an electric shock through my heart. My blood starts to boil, then rushes through my whole body. So that's what she thought of me?

That's... that's really sweet.

"Really?"

She nods, without losing her beautiful smile.

"Yes. He was a bit snide around the edges, but... I didn't mind. Besides, he seemed sincere."

"You have to beware of appearances."

"Apparently so."

The attraction between us is palpable, but neither of us takes the first step. It's as if we're standing on the edge of a precipice, hesitating to jump.

"And... do you think he has dreams, this Anderson?" she asks.

I can't help shaking my head. What kind of question is that? Any dreams? Of course, dreams. Will they come true? Well...

"Oh, well... I think Anderson would like to hit the road in a refurbished old van and drive around the West Coast looking for the best wave to ride."

She seems to like it. Could it be that she's as understanding as she seems? When I talked about doing this kind of road trip with Betty, she laughed in my face and talked about having children instead. Not that I'm against it. Of course I want children. But not prisoners of a deadly education that pushes us to bury everything we hold dear just to keep up appearances and business. That's not the way I see things.

"Sounds like a great plan. Doesn't he have anyone to go with him in this dream?"

Is she offering me something?

I'm in a panic. Shit, man.

"It's late, I'd better take you home," I finally say, breaking the spell of the moment.

She nods wordlessly.

We set off again, the car gliding silently through the deserted streets. When we arrive in front of her house, Elena turns to me.

"Thank you for everything, Matthew. Tonight was... different."

"Yes, different," I repeat, searching for the right words that don't come.

"In the future, maybe we should try talking to each other, instead of spitting at each other or threatening each other. Anyway, you saved me from the rain, so..."

"I agree to try and talk to each other," I nod.

She gets out of the Mustang, looking satisfied, and turns on her heels towards the entrance to her building. Then she stops, returns to the car and leans out of the window.

"Or... we don't talk. How about a nightcap in my apartment?"

Now I understand exactly what she's getting at and I like it. I know I shouldn't. Elena is a real drug. I've extended this evening to spend time with her and now it's her turn to play her cards to make me want to stay longer. It's like we're two teenagers who've just hooked up and are still trying to tame each other. I feel like I'm back in my younger days, and I find that rather exhilarating.

"A nightcap, huh?"

"You know what I mean, don't you? There are formulations for everything. It's just... rhetoric."

A rather determined and synthetic mind, I see. I like that very much. I'm a bit like that.

After parking the car, we drive up to her place together. And, of course, like all gracious and - usually - super-maniacal hosts, she warns me:

"Sorry, it's a bit of a mess."

Most people who say this usually have three peanuts lying around on the living-room coffee table, and a book that's been disturbed because they were reading it. All in all, it's nothing to compare their apartment to an absolute mess. But in Elena's case, I must admit I'm surprised. She's much messier than I'd imagined!

The apartment isn't upside down, but it's not tidy. There are clothes strewn all over the place, and it seems she doesn't much like cooking, judging by the number of takeaways that have been eaten here.

"Okay, I admit it's a mess," I confess.

"I warned you."

Maybe I'll put the 'synthetic' spirit aside. Elena is a dreamer. She craves passion and adventure. At the same time, it's hard not to understand her, when she spends most of her time surrounded by books. Inevitably, it gives her a taste for travel and thrills. That's what she's looking for.

"Well, now that we're here?"

Instead of immediately getting down to business, Elena hands me a glass, which she fills to the brim with red wine.

"Easy, on the dose. Do you want me to go home in one piece or not?"

"We'll see if you go home."

"Excellent point."

Neither of us really dares broach the subject, and yet I can see it in her eyes: we shouldn't be here, with each other. It's too dangerous and too... weird for us. But there's this irrepressible force, this attraction that makes me want to take her in my arms, lift her up, put her on that worktop and look after her in the best way I know how.

But again, I think that would be a little premature.

"We had a very interesting conversation about Anderson's dreams. But what about Elena's dreams?"

Suddenly, she blushes, as if she hasn't expected my question and is embarrassed by it.

"I'm... I'm not as comfortable talking about it as you are."

"Oh, well, why don't you talk about your friend's... Colette. What do you think?"

She looks up at me, a frank smile on her lips.

"Great idea, Mustang."

"So, what does Colette dream of?"

Elena moistens her lips in the wine glass, then lets the beverage swirl, so that it licks the sides. She seems lost in deep, intense thought.

"Colette, eh?" she begins in a dreamy voice. "Colette dreams of travel, of faraway adventures. She imagines exploring unknown cities, discovering different cultures, meeting fascinating people."

Her eyes light up, and I can almost see Colette's dreams - or rather, Elena's - come to life in her eyes.

"She also dreams of one day writing her own book. A story that would bring together all her experiences and encounters. A story that would inspire people to follow their dreams, no matter how crazy they may seem."

I listen, captivated by her enthusiasm. Elena, or Colette, has a passion that shines through every word. It's contagious, and I find myself imagining these journeys, these stories. Our dreams seem to be in tune...

"And you, Elena, what are your dreams?" I dare to ask, slightly breaking the thin wall between Colette and her.

She puts down her glass, staring at me with a serious expression.

"My dreams are almost the same. I've always wanted to travel, to see the world. But above all, I dream of writing. To immortalize my thoughts, my emotions, my adventures, even the smallest ones, in words."

I love that she recognizes it.

There's a vulnerability in her voice, as if she were revealing an intimate part of herself to me.

"Well, maybe it's time to start," I suggest gently. "I bet you've already got a whole bunch of stories in your head, ready to be told. No ?"

She smiles, a smile tinged with hope and reverie.

"Maybe you're right. Maybe it's time to start making those dreams come true. After all, I work in a bookstore, so..."

"Yes," I laugh. "It would be silly not to."

We stand in silence for a moment, each of us absorbed in our own thoughts. There's something magical about this moment, a subtle connection born of mutual understanding of our deepest wishes. We match each other, and that scares me as much as it pleases me.

Finally, Elena stands up, determined.

"For now, let's start by finishing this bottle of wine," she says with a wink.

I laugh, rising to join her. This evening, unexpected and complicated, turns into a moment of sincere, deep sharing. Despite all the complications, there's something real between us, something that goes beyond work colleagues or a one-night stand. It's the beginning of something new, something unexpected, but perhaps necessary. I feel I need it. I need to get away from this daily grind that's weighing me down, and every time a moment presents itself with Elena, I'm like a madman.

"I guess you're right."

What next? Come what may...

10

Elena

Note to self for the future: offering wine when you can't hold your liquor isn't a great idea. I'll stick it on a Post-it somewhere, just so I don't forget it the next time I get the chance. Even though my fingertips are tingling, for the moment I'm holding out and it's not unpleasant to feel a little freer from the stress that's been crushing me for the last few days.

"What's up? What do we do now? By the way... you know, I live a couple of blocks from here?" he says.

His smile is so enticing... and the way he swirls the wine in his glass. It's... rah... I hate myself for thinking like this, but it's just irresistible. He's standing in my living room and I'm so ashamed of the mess. Too ashamed, in fact. I offered to let him stay with me, but now I realize that was a bit suicidal of me.

I've just remembered that I've got a whole pile of clothes spread out on the bed, and garbage too - not that I'm dirty, mind you, but I do like to eat in bed, and it's not as if today meant I could go home and clean up.

"I'll tell you what. Maybe we should go back to your place, then."

But what am I proposing?

"What? Why's that?" he asks suspiciously. "Are you hiding a body in your room?"

Thriller readers' joke, I guess.

At least I get a chuckle out of it. But it's not enough to make me forget my idea. I've got to get him the hell out of here. What the hell was I thinking offering him a nightcap? I was afraid he wouldn't, so I decided to do it for him.

"It could be, yes."

"So, seriously? What's going on here?"

He's got this laugh on his face and I'm under his spell. I can't show him this side of me. Not at the moment. Tidying up the apartment has completely slipped my mind, and I feel like I'm being the biggest jerk right now.

"I don't have any condoms," I say.

My remark raises his eyebrows.

"If you like, I can go and buy some just around the corner from..."

"No. No, no, no, no. Let's go to your place. It'll be easier."

Matthew frowns and plants his gaze in mine, before nodding.

"All right, Woodstock. But I'm taking the bottle and leaving the car here. So, take care of it, okay? I'll come back for it tomorrow, with you."

Pfff. Out of the woods.

Not only am I relieved because I don't have to show him all the mess in my room - or my bathroom - but we're also strolling the streets with a good bottle of wine, which we share at the neck as we walk. How nice. Once again, I feel like a teenager, discovering alcohol and nightlife.

"Nice dreams, by the way," he says, taking the bottle from my hand to drink.

"Thanks," I laugh. "You too, that's not bad."

"I'm going to pursue mine. It's only a matter of time, you know. I have no intention of rotting in this bookstore for the rest of my life. Besides, it's not run at all the way I'd like it to be."

"Really? What do you mean?"

Matthew shrugs, then shoots a can that's lying around.

"You wouldn't think it, but I'm a big reader and I really like books. The object, I mean. It's a passion that comes from my mother."

I can't help smiling.

"She must be awfully proud that you've got a good job in a bookstore."

"Actually, she's... she's not really here anymore, you know?"

I remain silent for a few moments, aware that I've just thrown a spanner in the works.

"Sorry," he laughs softly, "I know it's not very glamorous and it can be a little chilling. Especially when we were just talking about condoms! Anyway, my father took off and my mother couldn't stand it. I do have a bit of family, but not here. They're in Colorado. I'm unattached."

Poor thing. It can't be easy.

"And... uh... you..."

"Live it well? Oh, yeah, it's fine," he retorts with a shrug. "I'm used to the solitude. It's always a bit hectic in my head. Sometimes I wonder what I've done to deserve this. But fortunately, I've got surfing. That relaxes me. It lets me forget all my worries. And then, of course, there are my friends. I'm sure you'd love them. They're like family to me. And then, before... there was the bookstore."

I know what he means. I imagine he thought of the people there as a second family. Except, since he's no longer with Betty, it must be very different.

"How did it go with Betty?"

I venture to ask this question. I sense that he's open to discussion, and that's lucky. The rain starts again, but only lightly. It's a drizzle. We don't even care. In fact, it's quite refreshing.

"Well, from a family point of view, of course, it wasn't bad. She has more cousins than I have fingers. So, family reunions were really lively. That was a positive thing. I felt less alone. But on the other hand, I realized that I was still alone and that she had a hold on me. And I'm not the kind of man to put up with that.

He's a loner, a bit wild, a bear, and unattached. Okay, I get it. I'm not much different, so I can't blame him.

We finally arrive at Matthew's and head upstairs.

"Well, you're lucky I let a stranger into my home. Normally... nobody comes here. It's kind of my haven."

As I enter Matthew's apartment, I'm immediately struck by the contrast between its rugged exterior and the gentle intimacy of his home. The apartment is spacious and surprisingly tidy, with minimalist yet warm decor. Bookshelves filled with books cover an entire wall, testifying to his passion for reading. A comfortable sofa faces a large window offering an impressive view of the city.

"Wow, it's... it's great here," I comment, amazed.

"Thank you," he replies, closing the door behind us. "This is my own little corner. I like to have a place where I can relax, away from the noise and bustle."

I notice a desk with a computer and several stacks of manuscripts. A surfboard leans against a corner, its wood gleaming in the subdued light. Photos of beaches and waves adorn the walls, and I can guess a passion for the ocean.

He's much more complex than I imagined. He's not only sexy, he's also... talented.

"Did you take these photos?" I ask, pointing to the pictures.

"Yeah, I love photography. Especially when it comes to capturing the ocean. It's another way for me to escape."

Matthew approaches the kitchen and opens another bottle of wine.

"Would you like a drink?"

"Yes, I'd love to. But we'll end up rolling under the table, won't we?"

He joins me with two glasses of wine, and we toast in silence. The mood is relaxed, almost peaceful. I feel strangely at ease, as if this place were familiar to me.

"So, tell me more about yourself, Woodstock. We're going to have to warm things up a bit because I've given you the cold shoulder. Sorry again about that. Anyway, I'm glad you like it here. And unlike you, I won't mind showing you my room."

I tilt my head to the side, embarrassed.

"I'm sorry... but I couldn't. I... it's all a bit too much of a mess for my taste. And... since you've 'made my day', I didn't have time to go home and tidy up. In the end, it's kind of your fault, you know."

Matthew bursts out laughing.

"I'm so sorry! But I didn't want the situation to get any worse. Or get out of hand. It would be horrible for us at the bookstore."

Yes, of course, he's right. Ideally, we shouldn't even see each other. This is already a big mistake. We're playing with fire here, and I have no doubt that we'll end up burning ourselves out if we carry on like this. But I want to get burned. When I see him. When my eyes pass over his and our gazes catch in that perfect harmony charged with desire, I want only one thing more: to burn. To burst into flames and become a human torch. Because, even though we hardly know each other, I feel I'm living a passion hotter than ever. Matthew is sometimes nice, sometimes unbearable. He blows hot and cold all the time, never giving me the slightest respite. I think, in a way, I like it.

"Because of *her*?"

He nods laconically. Suddenly, he's no longer laughing. On

the contrary, he's becoming serious. Matthew hates talking about Betty. You can tell right away. He can barely stand the mention of her name or her existence.

"Yeah. I don't want any more trouble."

She seems to have really given him a hard time.

"But what has she done to you?" I dare to ask.

I feel like I'm talking to a wounded kitten. It's quite a break from the image of the flirtatious, *bad-boy* type. Here, Matthew looks vulnerable for a change. He's showing his more... sensitive side.

"I'm not one to talk about my life, Woodstock."

"I'm not the type to go to strangers' houses. Or my *boss'*."

"I see. We're both out of our comfort zones, then."

I nod in support, then he takes a deep breath.

"When I came here, I was alone. It wasn't easy for me. I was from Colorado and had always dreamed of the beach and surfing. Anyway, no one was really waiting for me out there. I'd decided to live what we foolishly call the 'American dream'. That is, to become who I really wanted to be. Absolute freedom. That's what I'm attached to."

So far, I'm with him. I can see myself in his words. Following Kate was a bit of an American dream for me, after all. Even if, sometimes, when I see how she meddles in my private life, I regret it a little - because I want to kill her.

"So, I made some friends. And it was really cool, you know? I lived without thinking too much about anything else. I thought... maybe I was a bit lonely, but at least I was free. Unattached."

When he says these words, he has a twinkle in his eye. I can't even imagine how many chicks he must have squeezed during that period. It must be mind-blowing. I'm even a little jealous - when I shouldn't be.

Hateful feeling, get out of here!

108

"Yeah, I get it. You must have felt free."

"Totally. Then one day, while surfing, I met Betty. Honestly, we didn't hit it off right away, but something just clicked. I can't really explain it. I felt like I was in *Beauty and the Tramp*[4] . Except that I was the tramp. And it didn't matter. I did my utmost to find her, even when she was with her family and wasn't supposed to see me. It became a habit. I took all the risks for her."

It's kind of cute. I had no idea Matthew had such a soft heart. I don't want to cut it. He looks at his feet, then raises his head in my direction, his gaze more determined.

"Then things started to go wrong. Betty was crazy about me and I wanted to settle down. I'd been living from day to day for over a year. She offered me a job in her family's business. That's how I got a good job at the bookstore. Not least when she realized I was a great reader. At first, she thought I was her trophy: a simple surfer with concrete abs. She didn't think I was the slightest bit intellectual; can you imagine?"

Basically, I wouldn't have bet on this side of his personality either. Good for Betty, I guess.

I shrug my shoulders, just so I don't show it and keep Matthew confused. I'd hate to admit to him that I thought exactly the same as she did the first time I saw him. I think it would make him very uncomfortable and that's not the point. Especially when he's opening up and I'm finally learning more about him.

"It is said that clothes don't..."

"It's okay," he laughs, "I know you thought the same thing when you saw 'Anderson'."

"I saw that you were cultured," I exclaim.

"And is that what you were thinking when you stayed for that drink with me and then got into my car?"

---

4 *Disney cartoon from 1955.*

Touché...

Well, no, I was thinking more about his good looks, his dream body and, above all, I wanted to find out more about him. I wasn't at all interested in the fact that he knew thriller writers inside out, or that he read the Steinbeck classics[5] .

I moisten my lips, then swallow a swig of wine to try not to answer and let him continue.

"Betty seemed to have spotted potential in me and, I think you've gathered, she's an exceptional *businesswoman*. When she smells a lead, she doesn't let go until it's exploited. And that seam was me. In less than two months, I'd swapped afternoons with friends and evenings at the beach for family dinners in suits and brunches. In a way, life was smiling on me, but little by little, it began to pull me away from the people I cared about and deprive me of freedom. It may sound silly, but it quickly became suffocating. I was trapped in this situation to an extent you can't even imagine."

Her voice changes. It's no longer so assured. The timbre he employs reveals internal cracks.

"What do you mean by that?" I ask softly.

"When it's someone else who oversees your whole world, Elena, she practically has the right of life and death over you. Without you even realizing it. She can control you down to the smallest detail. She plans your life, and you feel as if her decisions are your own. You feel like... a prisoner and a volunteer at the same time. You know you could leave, but you don't want to. Because it's too hard. Because it's become too comfortable to live on autopilot."

And one fine day...

"And then it all fell apart," he adds.

This time, Matthew looks grim. There's nothing left of the slightly snide, bewildering guy I know. He's like... transformed.

---

5 *American writer who won the Nobel Prize for Literature in 1962.*

It's as if a dull rage has taken hold of his whole being, tensing every muscle in his body.

"That was one time too many. So, I decided to leave. I've broken free of my shackles, but not completely either. Let's just say... I'm still handcuffed. I still work at the bookstore and have to put up with her and her stupid brother."

His story resonates with me. It speaks to me more than he imagines...

Now I understand the whole story, too. It's the stigma of this life of control that still prevents Matthew from asserting himself to Betty and living out a new relationship. He knows she's a perfidious manipulator of the worst kind who wouldn't hesitate to destroy him and his new conquest.

And that conquest could be me...

I put myself in a trickier situation than I'd imagined. But now that I've put my finger in the machine, it's hard to get out. Especially if I stay at the bookstore. But damn it, I need this job. If I don't have this, I can't pay my rent and live here. It would be... back to square one: New York, or Connecticut with my parents, and I don't want that at all. I want to live my life. I, too, crave adventure and freedom.

Matthew claps his hands gently, then looks at me, resuming his mysterious, laughing look.

"Did I do it?" he asks.

"Do what?"

"Definitely killed the party?"

I smile. If he thinks I'm out of it, he's wrong!

"Oh no! You see, you've just fed my nurse syndrome and now... I feel terribly attracted to you."

Did I just fucking say that out loud?

Instead of asking me to leave his house because I'm a weird girl who forgets all her filters when she's had a bit to drink, Matthew looks at me warily, then bursts out laughing, before taking another sip of wine.

When that's done, he refills both of our glasses to finish the bottle. This is it, we're going to be drunk as hell, and in this situation, I can't answer for anything. I don't usually drink. What's the matter with me, getting all worked up over this guy? I don't recognize myself. Everything's moving so fast in my feelings for him, it's worrying me. When he talked about one person who can control our whole world and probably make it rain or shine... I'm so afraid that's going to happen to me one day.

I think I'm really falling for his innocent charm. Because that's what Matthew is. But he's also a well-built man, with a confident charisma and a swaying gait, who's moving in my direction with an air of determination.

Oh, no, damn it, I can't break down like that. I've got to make him understand that it's not a sure thing.

Just as he's about to put his hands on me, I stop him dead in his tracks. He opens his mouth to protest, but I counter-attack again, smothering his words with the tip of my index finger.

"What the hell are you doing?" he articulates with my finger on his lips.

"I'll make you wait."

I think it's not quite me, but the wine, talking. That said, Matthew doesn't seem to mind. Quite the opposite, in fact. His face is first crossed with astonishment, then he seems interested in the game I'm proposing.

" I don't think you're gonna make it, Woodstock."

My heart beats a little faster and a little louder. I pray he can't hear it squarely through the tiles, so vigorously is it drumming in my chest. Maybe he's right. I'm not going to make it.

But I'll give it a try.

"This time I won't lose, my dear Mustang. You see, I haven't forgotten what you did to me in the storeroom earlier, and... I didn't appreciate it. Not at all."

"You looked it, though."

With every word, he baffles me.

"You didn't finish the job. And do you know what we do to employees who don't finish the job?"

"Are we asking them to work overtime and finish during the night?"

"Exactly," I say. "All night long."

"I like that plan."

I smile, pleased with myself. I manage to impose a little control. Because, if I let myself, I think I could let Matthew take me right there, right now, on the couch. That would probably be just as well, but if we're going to have a working relationship, or... a bit more, I want it to be balanced. I'm learning from my mistakes too, and I won't be anyone's submissive anymore. I've already had an engagement fall apart because of a manipulative control freak. It won't happen again. Matthew and I almost have a similar story. I intend to make the best of it. On both sides.

So, I ask Matthew to sit down on one of the armchairs in the living room so I can take care of him. And this time, I don't intend to go easy on him. I'm going to heat him up so much he'll be boiling.

I start by taking off my top. His eyes become as round as marbles.

"Okay, this plan just keeps getting better and better," he murmurs.

"You haven't seen anything yet."

I decide to give him everything he's been waiting for, so he won't believe it. I want to drive him crazy. And for that, there's nothing better than to slowly strip naked, under his eager gaze.

"Fuck, Elena, you're going to drive me crazy if you keep

this up."

"That's the whole point," I say as I finish undressing.

Matthew looks more and more interested, but every time he wants to touch me, I push him away. I'm not going to give in that easily. The goal is to get him to beg me in the end, and I think it won't be long before he does.

The tension in the room is palpable, electric. Every movement, every gesture is charged with an unspoken promise, a simmering expectation. Matthew looks at me, his desire clearly visible in his eyes - and elsewhere - but he plays by the rules, waiting for my go-ahead.

Finally, after what seems like an eternity, I give in. I move closer to him, our bodies brush against each other, and I feel his breath quicken. Our lips meet in a passionate kiss, a mixture of sweetness and fever. It's a moment of pure abandon when the rest of the world seems to disappear.

I soon find myself straddling him, his stiff cock leaving the shackles of his pants and rubbing against my intimacy. There's no need for foreplay, we're so excited by each other. Before I can finish settling in, he penetrates me with a thrust of his pelvis, causing me to cry out in surprise and pleasure.

Damn, this guy's divine, and all over the place...

We then embark on a wild ride, leaving us sweaty and panting. But the night has clearly just begun...

* * *

Morning comes too quickly. I wake up in Matthew's arms, the sun filtering through the curtains. I'm a little lost, my head full of memories of last night. It was intense, passionate, but now I don't know where it's going to lead.

Well done. And to think I wasn't supposed to give in! It's just terrible. I'm still overwhelmed by what I've just done.

I tiptoe out of bed, trying not to wake him. I gather my clothes from the floor and dress quickly. I take one last look at Matthew, who's sleeping peacefully, then leave the apartment.

In the cool of the morning, I walk alone, my thoughts swirling. What happened last night was incredible, but I'm torn between desire and fear of what it means for the future. I'm afraid of getting too attached too quickly, afraid of the complexity of our relationship at work, afraid of losing myself in this budding passion.

I can never find a good person. I don't think I can. Would he be the one? No, he couldn't be. He's my superior! I just can't do it.

But one thing's for sure, I can no longer ignore my feelings for Matthew. They have arrived as firmly as I feared.

I have to find a way to deal with this situation, to understand what I really want. For now, I need to focus on the day ahead, trying to keep my mind clear, despite the whirlwind of emotions that's overtaking me.

I really am the queen of stupid!

11

Matthew

Shit, what the hell was that night? Just as I turn to take
Elena in my arms, I realize she's gone. Usually, I'm the one
who sneaks out in the wee hours of the morning.

I lay there for a moment, staring at the empty space beside me, the sheets still crumpled from our night together. A
strange feeling runs through me. I'm torn between surprise
and a touch of regret.

What the hell am I doing...

I shouldn't have done it. If Betty knew, she'd kill me and
Elena. But it was a magical evening. Our aspirations seem
strangely similar.

I can't get back into a relationship. Usually, it's one night
stand after another. I'm not the type to get attached like that,
at least not now. The truth is, I don'twant t o. If I go down that
road, I might not come back unscathed, and I don't want that.
I've already taken enough.

I stand up, staring around my apartment, almost hoping
to find her still here, somewhere. But no, she's gone, leaving
behind a silence that weighs heavily.

I head to the kitchen to make myself a cup of coffee and my
thoughts become muddled. Last night was incredible, intense,
a real connection. But now, in the clarity of the morning, I

wonder what this means for us. Have I crossed a line? And if so, how are we going to handle this at work?

I'm her boss.

As I sip my coffee, I recall every detail of the evening, every smile, every touch. It was different from anything I've ever known, deeper, more real. But that makes it more complicated.

And sex. God, the sex. It was awesome. She really drove me crazy.

I know I have to talk to her. We need to clarify things, understand where we stand. It's not going to be easy. Working relationships mixed with feelings are always tricky. I know all about that. Anyway, it's the weekend. I'll wait for her to get back to me. She's got my number after all. I think she should do it soon.

Normally...

I finish my coffee, determined to face the day. There's a mixture of excitement and apprehension in me. I have the feeling that Elena and I have embarked on something unique, but I'm not sure how to navigate these uncharted waters. The more I hang out with her, the more I get into trouble. We need to define what happened between us and where it leads. Whatever the outcome, I know I can't ignore how I feel about her.

It's uncharted territory, but I'm ready to explore.

I'm ready to forget Betty.

* * *

Today, it's a surf day with Anton and Derek. The weekend, the best time of the week, no doubt about it! But even though I'm supposed to be having fun, I keep Elena on my mind. She never leaves my mind. I can't get her out of my mind.

Shit...

On the way to the beach, I try to concentrate on the day ahead, on the waves, the sun and the sand. But my thoughts keep drifting back to Elena, to that night we spent together, and all the implications it carries.

Why can't I forget her for a moment? And why doesn't she contact me?

I glance at my phone, but still nothing.

Anton and Derek quickly notice that I'm not quite myself.

"Hey, man, you seem out of it today. Is everything okay?" asks Derek, giving me a friendly pat on the back.

I grab my board and pull it out of the van, shaking my head.

"Yeah, I'm okay. Just a little concerned, I guess," I retort, trying to sound more enthusiastic.

I can't lie. Not to them.

"Heart trouble, eh?" Anton guesses with a mischievous smile.

I sigh. These guys know me too well.

"Maybe," I say at last. "It's complicated."

"Betty, huh? She's such a bitch. You should definitely cut her loose. You know, we saw what she did to you. It's like she sucked all the joy out of you! You're not going to let that happen, are you?"

They have no idea how much. They only know part of the story. That said, it's not because of Betty.

"Are you waiting for a message, or what?" insists Derek.

"No, no..."

I have to say that I check my phone every two minutes. It's almost compulsive now. It sucks.

We reach the beach, and I force myself to concentrate on surfing. The cold water, the wind in my hair, the rhythm of the waves, all help to clear my mind, at least temporarily.

But even as I surf, balancing my body on the board, letting myself be carried away by the waves, the image of Elena invades my mind. Her presence seems to inhabit me, influencing every thought, every movement.

Should I see her after hours? I'm not sure.

After a few hours in the water, we sit down on the sand, tired but satisfied. Anton and Derek share beers and stories, but I feel distracted. It's not worth it to extricate myself from Betty's negative influence and fall back into my old ways, tying myself down again.

"You should talk to her, man," Anton advises me, noticing my lack of participation in the conversation.

"To Betty? No, definitely not," agrees Derek.

"Listen," I confess, "it's not her I'm thinking about. There's another girl."

They both look at me with such astonished expressions that I feel as if I've uttered an enormity.

"Wait, what? You're telling us there's a girl you like? Other than Betty?"

I prefer not to answer. Then, inevitably, Anton resumes: "Where's our Matt'?"

"Yeah, I know, I know. I think I'm making a mistake."

The rest of the day passes in a haze of reflection. I realize that I can't ignore my feelings for Elena. What happened between us has changed something, and it's time to face that reality.

Standing on my board, feeling the constant movement of the waves beneath me, I feel at peace. Surfing, for me, is more than a sport: it's an escape, a way to free myself from my emotions, to feel connected to something bigger than myself. Each wave is a new challenge, a new chance to feel alive, really alive. To forget all the problems of everyday life.

I look off into the distance, spotting a promising wave. I row towards it, my heart beating to the rhythm of the water lapping around me. As I approach, I rise in one fluid motion, finding my balance almost instinctively. The wave carries me, and I melt into its energy, leaving all my worries behind.

Anton and Derek can't believe it. I always blow their minds.

The wind blows through my hair, the water gushes around me, and for a moment, I'm completely free. Free of my thoughts, free of my worries, free of Elena's hold on my mind. But as I continue to glide along my board, an image of my beautiful colleague creeps into my mind. Her smile, her laughter, the feel of her skin against mine... I lose my focus, my balance wavers. All this distracts me, and in an instant, I'm falling.

Fuck!

The force of the wave seizes me. For a brief moment, I'm disoriented, back underwater. It's a brutal reminder of reality. No matter how much I feel in control, there are always unexpected elements that can surprise me.

I surface, catching my breath. I'm dripping, a bit stunned too, but mostly, I'm struck by my situation. Even here on the water, where I feel freest, I can't escape Elena.

Why does she have such an effect on me? I hardly know her! Well, apart from the physical aspect...

As I head back to the beach, Anton and Derek rush towards me.

"You okay, man? You've never fallen like that before!"

"Yeah. I'm good. I'm good. Just something to take care of, I guess."

I have to get rid of these parasitic thoughts.

★ ★ ★

Not a single message all weekend. Not a call, to talk about what happened between us or just to say hello...

Say hello? Are you serious, man?

I'm waiting, and nothing. I understand what's happening. I fall into the arms of yet another girl who, deep down, doesn't give a damn about me. All she wants is to have sex for free. As nice as it is, if I let myself, I'll end up with another would-be Betty on my back. That's not an option. I've got to protect myself. In the end, maybe it's better that we don't see each other outside of work. Yes, it's better that way.

I put my keys in the special bowl in the hallway, then settle into my sofa with a sigh.

Shit, I've gotten myself into a bad situation again and I'm going to have a hard time getting out of it.

On the other hand, as much as I'd like to forget it, there's the memory of our diabolical embrace. Of our bodies becoming one. It was such a hot, *hot, hot* moment. How can I not think about it? In the morning, my sheets were a mess, as if a storm had passed over them. It was crazy. There's a connection between us that I can't even begin to define, it's so deep and powerful. Elena and I are attracted to each other. That's all there is to it. I don't know what more to say about her. And the more 'forbidden' she is, the more I want her. Suddenly, I understand Eve, when she was ordered not to bite into the apple but did it anyway. Of course it's tempting. Especially when the fruit is as appetizing as it is forbidden!

It's a call I'm not sure I can resist...

Sundays are for rest, but also for sport, at the gym. When I have time, I train every day. But lately things have been a bit... hectic.

When Monday finally arrives, I'm nervous, but I know what I have to do: absolutely nothing. I go to work with the idea of showing nothing of what I'm feeling and being perfectly cool with Elena. It's not against her - yeah, well, a bit, she hasn't bothered to text me, and neither have I really... - but I have to protect myself and make sure I still keep my job. I need it to finish my project and take off with my van. And we're both going to suffer for sure, and I don't want that.

As I walk towards the bookstore, I mentally prepare myself to ignore her, to pretend that nothing has happened between us. It's painful, but necessary. I can't afford to let my feelings interfere with my work or my peace of mind.

I push open the bookstore door and the first thing I see is her. There she is, behind the counter, putting away books. She looks up at me and our eyes meet. I feel a spark, a shiver, but I stifle it immediately.

"Hey, Matthew, you..."

I won't answer.

I head for my office without a word, without another glance at her. It's hard, harder than I thought, but it's the only way to put an end to it. I settle down at my desk, immersing myself in work to forget, to protect myself.

I don't know how long I can maintain this distance, this facade of indifference, but I'm determined to try. For my well-being, for my future, I must keep Elena at a distance, however painful it may be.

Damn Betty, who decided to make us work together for this damn event. I don't think I'll be able to do it without cracking, and I have no desire for these work sessions to turn into intense, torrid fuck sessions.

Oh yes... Hot fucking...

The morning passes slowly, each minute seeming like an eternity. I try to concentrate on my work, on the papers piling up on my desk, but my mind is constantly distracted. I sneak glances at Elena when I pass her, making sure she's busy, far away from me.

I mustn't think about it.

Every time I go out for a coffee, I'm unlucky enough to see her, and every time our eyes meet by chance, I quickly avert my gaze. I know that if I gaze into hers for too long, I risk losing myself and giving in to temptation. It's a dangerous game, a precarious balance I'm trying to maintain.

When lunchtime comes, I decide to go out and clear my head. I walk aimlessly through the streets, losing myself in my thoughts. I'm angry with myself for letting things go this far with her, for not keeping a cool head.

Now I'm in trouble.

When I get back to the bookstore, I force myself to remain professional, to treat Elena like any other colleague. But it's difficult. Every word I say, every gesture I make, is charged with an unspoken meaning, a repressed desire.

Without warning, she finally burst into my office, looking furious.

"How long are you going to play this game?"

Shit...

"What do you want? And I don't know what you're talking about."

Elena sits down across from me, as if invited.

"You ignore me completely."

"I'm not ignoring you, but we're at work."

Liar. Big liar. Does she have to be so fucking sexy today on purpose?

How could I ignore her when she seems to radiate an irresistible aura? Her outfit accentuates her natural charm in an almost unbearable way. She's wearing a simple, fitted dress that delicately accentuates her curves. The red color of the dress perfectly complements her complexion, adding a touch of freshness to her already captivating appearance.

Her chestnut hair falls loosely around her shoulders, giving her look a casual yet well-groomed air. And her green eyes shine with a sparkle that seems to pierce me every time our eyes meet.

I hate her. I can't resist her.

I try to look away, to concentrate on something other than his chest, but to no avail. Her presence is like a magnet, irresistibly drawing my attention. Every gesture, every movement she makes seems designed to capture my gaze, to remind me of what happened between us.

I must admit, reluctantly, that Elena has the power to destabilize me, just by the way she looks, by her appearance, which today seems designed to torment me. It's a constant struggle to keep my mind focused on my work and not on her, on this burning desire she awakens in me.

"By the way," I say after clearing my throat, "your outfit isn't regulation. You'll have to go home and change."

She makes big eyes, then looks at me, offended.

"What are you talking about?"

"It's unprofessional. That's all there is to it. So, come back with a suitable outfit and the hour you spend changing will be deducted from your salary."

Furious, Elena bangs her fist on my desk.

"I'm sick of you, Matthew, Anderson, Mustang, or whatever I'm supposed to call you! You're always like this! One minute you're hot, the next you're cold."

"If you don't know how to be professional, that's not my problem."

I have a feeling I'm going too far. Elena is bubbling over inside. It's clear she hates me, and I deserve it. I've got to get her away from me. If I don't, I'll embarrass myself again, and if I have to choose, I'll have to put my dream ahead of my affection for her.

"You're a really... you're a really horrible guy, you know that?"

I'm cracking up.

"Not a single text message. Not a thing. Not one call."

125

She straightens up, as if she's just been shocked.

"Oh, I see. So that's it?" she hisses. "Is that why you're giving me the silent treatment? Well, what about you? Have you been trying to contact me?"

Touché.

"I'm not having a fit," I retort in a lower voice. "But I think we could have discussed it."

"What's there to talk about?"

"What we're going through. You can see it's not normal!"

"And it bothers you that much?"

I don't answer her question. Of course not, I don't mind. Of course, I want more because I'm so drawn to her."

But I can't. *I mustn't.*

"Well?" she insists.

"Yes," I finally say.

"What... what?"

We might as well drive the nail in.

"You didn't really think we'd end up together, did you, Woodstock? It's just sex, okay? And it's got to end. I'm not in the habit of sleeping with the same woman, multiple times."

I can see all the anger in her eyes. She expected more. She doesn't know how much this is costing me. She doesn't know that I'm really sacrificing what I'm beginning to feel for her by telling her this. But I also know that she'd end up being eaten alive by Betty. We couldn't hide our relationship for long. All this... it's too complicated. I'd rather keep her out of trouble. As much as I can handle it. I know Betty and I know how to defend myself. But in Elena's case... I can't be sure and I refuse to get her in trouble up to her neck. She needs this job. And so do I. I should just keep my distance from her.

"Is that all?"

"What, you thought there was more? You were naive. I got what I wanted, and now you can go. I don't really care. And if you tell anyone about this, I guarantee you'll have such a hard time that all you'll want to do is quit. I can make your life hell here. Trust me on that."

Elena has a sad look on her face. I think she's holding back from bursting into tears, and my heart cracks at the same time.

"Oh, I trust you, yes."

She turns on her heels, then, an hour later, returns in an outfit more appropriate for work. Gone is the dress. No more looks. We're content to work together on planning the event we've been asked to organize.

The afternoon passes in palpable tension. We exchange ideas and plans, but there's always this distance between us, an invisible wall that I've erected and that throws a damper on things.

I hate myself for doing this. And she probably hates me too. But it's for the best.

By the end of the day, I'm exhausted, not physically, but emotionally. I realize that this situation is not sustainable in the long term. I need to find a way to manage my feelings for Elena, to find a balance between my professional life and my personal desires.

I go home with a heavy heart, knowing that tomorrow will be another day of struggle, another day when I'll have to face Elena and everything she means to me. I wonder how long I can hold out before I give in, before I recognize how I really feel about her.

But in his interest, as in mine, we must leave it at that.

And for that, I have to be detestable.

12

Elena

I hate him. I don't have the slightest respect for him anymore, and he doesn't deserve it anyway. He's just a first-class jerk. Matthew is everything that turns me off in a man. Warm when he wants to get laid, he turns into a snow queen when it comes to talking about anything other than sex. If that's what he wants to play, then fine, I can play too. But shit, I thought there was more going on between us. I must have been kidding myself and I definitely have to draw a line under this budding relationship, which will obviously never see the light of day. It would be too complicated anyway.

I look like shit in front of my bedroom mirror. Kate won't stop yelling at me.

"What's the matter with you? It's Friday night and we have to go out for a drink. Come on! It's like I'm asking you to finish a math exam."

Ugh. Just thinking about it...

I can't tell Kate. She'd inevitably repeat it to Travis, who might repeat it to others, until it reached Betty's ears and that would be a disaster. Or even worse, my friend could come to my defense, and she'd go talk to Matthew, even if he's her superior. I'm sure he'd hate that with every fiber of his being and I don't want to trigger that kind of reaction in him.

Kate couldn't care less. Hierarchical superior or not, you don't touch your best friend - and that's also why I love her so much, my Kate - but in this case, it can only do me a disservice.

So, to the question: 'What's wrong with you at the end of the day?', I feel like answering: heartbreak. But I don't say anything. I also feel like crying because the guy I used to get along with turns out to be the worst kind of bastard who doesn't even care about me.

We spent the week ignoring each other, after fucking last weekend. And it doesn't make any sense! I'm fed up...

I shake my head, trying to chase away my negative thoughts. Tonight, I've got to get out, get my mind off things. I can't stay trapped in this bubble of sadness and frustration.

"I'm fine. Just a little tired, that's all."

She gives me a skeptical look, but doesn't push any further. She knows when to back off, my Kate. She's always there for me, but she also understands that sometimes I need my space.

I finish getting ready, putting on an outfit that gives me a little more confidence. Tonight, I want to forget Matthew, forget this story that never really began. I just want to be Elena, free and carefree, at least for a few hours.

"Come on! Let's make the most of this farewell party!"

"What's it for again?" I ask.

Kate looks almost annoyed that I've forgotten.

"Stephanie's maternity leave."

"Who's Stephanie? I'm pretty sure I've never seen this one before."

"You're really out of it these days."

Kate shakes her head, an indulgent smile on her lips, before taking me by the arm to lead me out of my apartment. I give in, knowing she's right. I need to get out, breathe, meet people and think about something else.

As I walk to the bar, I force myself to leave behind all

thoughts of Matthew, of this strange week at work. Tonight, I just want to enjoy the moment.

"I know there's something else," Kate says as we turn a corner. "Don't lie to me."

"What... what?"

She raises her eyes to the sky with a smile, then enunciates to me:

"You've got a lot of different 'I'm upset because I'm sulking' types, Elena. And I know them all."

Now she surprises me. But it's not true. At least, I think it isn't. I can't see my own face, but I'm sure she's still making up nonsense.

"Is Matthew going to be there?"

"Why are you asking me that? Do you have a crush on him or something?"

I don't answer, just keep as quiet as possible. If I'd shouted back, she'd certainly have suspected something. But after a few seconds of silence, I let out a laconic "no".

"Yeah, right. Liar! You're really taking me for a sucker, aren't you?"

"What are you imagining?"

"What am I imagining? No, what's more important is what's going on in that twisted little head of yours, girl, because I'm pretty sure you're dreaming about him and you on top of each other, in inappropriate places."

If, at that very moment, Kate knew how RIGHT she was...

But that doesn't have to be the case anymore. I've only been here a short time and I'm already under a guy's spell. It's hellish to have such a sensitive heart.

"Stop talking nonsense."

"Elena, I can see your looks, your little games of seduction and so on. I'm not stupid! And neither is Travis. It's starting to show."

131

Rha, shit!

All the more reason for it to stop immediately. I don't want any trouble, but beyond that, I don't want to cause him any.

"There's nothing between us, I assure you!"

My friend stops me dead in my tracks, then grabs me by the shoulders. Wow, what's wrong with her? She's rarely been so serious.

"Elena, listen to me. I don't want you to think: 'Oh, no, if Kate knows, she'll tell everyone, I can't trust her, etc.' Because that's not true. If I repeat things, it's because I know they have no consequences. But I would never willingly put you in trouble, you understand? We're like sisters, you and me. You can tell me anything."

The sincerity of her eyes, of her speech. OK... I let her have it, and almost immediately she breaks into a cheeky laugh.

"I knew it!" she exclaims.

"It's okay, don't say it so loud." It feels good to admit it to someone.

We continue on our way.

"Is it a good one?"

"Stop."

"Does he have a big one?"

"Stop it!"

She glues her index fingers together, then gently peels them apart.

"You stop me when we get to the size of his dick, okay?"

"Kate!"

"It's okay, it's okay."

By the time we reach the bar, the atmosphere is already lively. Stephanie, whom I finally recognize after a brief introduction, is radiant and surrounded by friends and colleagues. I catch myself smiling genuinely, happy for her. Everyone is there. Yes, everyone. *Even Matthew.*

My heart leaps into my chest when I see him. There he is, leaning against the bar, deep in conversation with a few colleagues. He looks relaxed, smiling, so different from the cold, distant man I've known at work these past few days.

Kate, who has followed my gaze, nudges me.

"It looks like someone's seen a ghost," she whispers.

"Shh, don't say anything," I murmur, trying to look away from Matthew.

But it's difficult. Every time my eyes drift to him, my heart speeds up. A mixture of frustration, desire and anger seizes me. I remember the moments we shared, the passion, but also the wall he's built between us since.

I take a deep breath, trying to concentrate on the evening, on the people around me, on Stephanie. But it's a losing battle. Matthew is like a magnet, drawing my attention in spite of myself.

"Would you like something to drink?" suggests Kate, drawing me out of my thoughts.

"Yes, a glass of wine, please," I say, grateful for the distraction.

As Kate walks away to fetch our drinks, I feel a little lost, alone with my conflicting thoughts and emotions. The evening becomes a challenge, a balancing act between wanting to enjoy the moment and fighting the irresistible attraction I feel for Matthew.

I promise myself to stay strong, not to give in, not to let him disrupt my evening. But deep down, I know it's a hard promise to keep. He's already left an indelible mark on my life, and I'm not sure I can erase it so easily.

"Come on," says my friend, returning with our drinks. "Forget about him, okay? He's just a guy."

I'm not answering.

"A guy with a huge one in his underpants, so be it! Well,

you stop my fingers when it's the right size, OK? I want to know!"

"Kate!"

"All right, all right, I'll *really* stop this time."

I swallow my glass almost in one gulp and can't think of anything else but the evening.

"Ray approaching," says Kate. "I repeat Ray approaching!"

Ray? What the hell does he want?

The handsome, impeccable-looking blond boy approaches us.

"Can I buy you a drink?" he asks. "I have a feeling yours is empty, and that's no way to spend a good evening."

I glance in Matthew's direction and see that he's looking at me. Then the thought crosses my mind. Oh, how bad I am. Oh, that's not good at all, but since that's the way it is, I'll give him a bit of a run for his money...

I'm going to make him so jealous.

"I'd love to!"

I turn to Ray, flashing a seductive smile. I'm aware that Matthew is watching us, but I do my best to ignore his burning gaze. Ray orders two drinks and starts talking, but I'm honestly only half listening. My mind is still cluttered with Matthew, with the complicated situation between us.

"Do you like the bookstore?"

"Yes, thank you very much."

"Well," says Kate, "I guess I'll leave you to it."

Ray's only response is a terse nod. He doesn't beat around the bush, and that's fine with me. If Matthew wants to play dumb, he'll understand that I can do more than he imagines, in this area.

"As far as I'm concerned, I run the stationery department," says Ray proudly. "It's a shame you like the bookstore so much, I'm sure you'd love my department too."

"Without a doubt, yes."

"If you like anything to do with writing and stuff, we've got notebooks, lots of different pens, well, you know. I'm a bit of a poet myself, and that gave me some ideas."

"Oh, really?" I'm just pretending.

I must not seem sufficiently interested in him. At the same time, our conversation is utterly banal. Then Ray starts declaiming some of his poems to me. I don't know if he's drunk, but one thing's for sure: he lacks talent.

"It's magnificent, bravo."

"Oh, thanks, but it's not much."

Strange that he should show a little modesty. I don't think that's what's suffocating him. I need to be more convincing to make Matthew mad. I know he's conflicted with Ray and I'll keep stoking the embers of jealousy.

I laugh at Ray's jokes, lean toward him to better hear him speak, play with my hair in a way I know is attractive. I can feel Matthew's eyes on us. He's pulling a three-meter-long face, and it gives me an unhealthy satisfaction.

I'm lost in this dangerous game, caught up in a dynamic of revenge and jealousy. It's a slippery slope, and I know it, but I can't stop myself from going on.

"The more you tell me about it, the more I think this department looks really great," I say.

Third glass. If I go on like this, I won't be able to stand up and answer for anything.

Ray seems delighted by my feigned enthusiasm and continues to talk about his work with a zeal that fails to capture my interest. I keep an eye on Matthew, trying to analyze his reaction, but it's hard to decipher.

I feel as if I'm on the edge, oscillating between the desire to lose myself in the evening to forget Matthew and the awareness that I'm playing a role that isn't really mine. Ray, with his one-way conversation, only accentuates this feeling.

At one point, I find myself wishing Matthew would come and save me from this endless conversation. But no, I quickly pull myself together. He won't decide my evening. I'm the master of my own decisions.

To make sure I stay in control, I decide to slow down on the alcohol. I don't want to find myself in a situation where I regret my actions. I refuse to be the victim of my own game.

"I think I'll call it a night on the booze," I say to Ray. "But thanks for the conversation."

He looks a little disappointed, but nods. I excuse myself politely and walk away, looking for some fresh air. As I move away, I take one last look at Matthew. Our eyes meet and I feel a spark, a shiver that runs down my spine.

I escape outside the bar, taking deep breaths. The coolness of the night soothes me, refocuses me. I realize that this evening has been more emotionally taxing than I had anticipated.

What's the matter with me, behaving like this?

On the other hand, I have a feeling it worked and Matthew was crazy with jealousy. It was... rather nice to see.

Kate joins me outside.

"Hey!"

"Hmm?"

"What are you playing at, gorgeous?" she asks.

"I... rah... I knew you'd see what was happening."

She nods with a reproving look on her face.

"Everyone sees it, in fact. Ray is openly hitting on you. You didn't think that would go unnoticed, did you?"

By way of reply, I shrug my shoulders, as if none of this matters to me.

"I know, I know... I shouldn't. But fuck, that's because Matthew... He doesn't give a shit about me, does he?"

"Not at all," she laughs. "In fact, he looked downright annoyed. Look, I'm not the best at love advice and I'm not sure I'm the best at it, but I think you should stop playing this little game, don't you? It's going to end badly and you know it."

She's right. On the other hand, I'm feeling a bit tipsy and I don't feel like letting Matthew win at all. He'd be too happy with the situation. I don't want that.

"I know, I know, I know. But if I'm not with Matthew, I've got a right to be with someone else, haven't I?"

Kate grimaces, as if I've just uttered an enormity.

"Someone else, yes, but maybe not Ray McGee, who is literally his own worst enemy. Can you imagine?"

"I don't care, Kate. He gives me a hard time at work, he's not clear with me... Trust me, he deserves what he gets."

"On that, I agree. But... Ray, really?"

"What's that? Underneath his first-class exterior, he's not bad."

"You don't care at all."

"No, no," I say in bad faith. "At least he cares about me. He's not afraid of what other people might think."

That's where I nail him.

"So, you're going to keep on playing, eh?"

"Better twice than once."

"I see," she laughs. "Well, OK, let's not get them to kill each other over your ass, shall we?"

I nod, then Kate re-enters the bar to 'have one more drink'. Come to think of it, almost all of us are drinking alcohol to celebrate the maternity leave of a woman who can no longer drink. How cruel!

Just as I decide to go back into the bar, Ray comes out to join me. Now I'd better be good.

He stands beside me, a confident smile on his lips. He holds up two glasses, offering me one of them.

"I thought you might need another drink," he says.

"Thanks, Ray. That's sweet," I retort, taking it.

I feel his gaze on me, heavy, full of expectation. I wonder if he realizes he's just a pawn in my game with Matthew. But maybe he wouldn't even mind. Ray always has this slightly overconfident, almost arrogant attitude. I don't know him well, but I see the way he is. And... he's clearly not the kind of man, usually, to whom you say 'no'. Or rather, the kind of man who accepts being told 'no'.

"Do you want to get away from this party?" he asks.

I look at him, weighing my words.

"Look, Ray, I... I just came here to have a good time, nothing serious."

He nods, but I can see a glimmer of hope in his eyes.

"Of course, of course. Just for fun."

I feel a little guilty playing with Ray's expectations, but I can't help looking back towards the bar entrance, hoping to catch a glimpse of Matthew.

He's not there. Maybe he's gone, or maybe he's watching me from the inside. I don't know, and that frustrates me.

"You know, Elena, I think you deserve better," he says suddenly.

I look at him, surprised.

"Better?"

"Yes. Someone who sees you for what you really are, not just as a game."

His words strike me. It's disturbing that he should say it like that. As if he had... knowledge of our relationship, with Matthew.

Have I gotten so lost in this game with Matthew that I've forgotten who I really am? Do I really deserve better, or am I just lying to myself?

"I saw how he looked at us, you know," he smiles. "You want to please him, don't you?" he advances proudly.

"What? No. No, I just..."

"No need to lie."

Well, OK. Obviously, we're not very discreet.

But the fact that Ray knows about this is a real problem.

"I'll be as silent as a grave, don't worry," he smiles.

I'm not sure I can trust him.

I say nothing more and decide to go back into the bar to get my coat. As I make my way through the crowd, I feel a weight in my stomach. The bar is noisy, people are laughing and dancing, but all I want is to escape, to be away from it all. This game is stupid after all. I'll make Matthew pay, that's for sure, but I don't know how yet. At least, not like this.

I head for the changing rooms, collect my coat and prepare to leave, when suddenly a hand grips my arm firmly. I turn to see Matthew, his face dark with anger.

"What do you think you're doing?" he scolds.

I'm caught off guard by his aggressive tone.

"I'm... I'm going home, Matthew. Why? Get your hands off me."

"Stop it, Elena. You think I don't see what you're doing? Are you playing with Ray just to make me jealous?"

His voice is laden with frustration and anger, and I can feel my own temper flaring.

"Maybe if you didn't act like such an asshole, I wouldn't have to..."

I stop, realizing that I'm about to reveal my feelings, my vulnerability.

"Have to what, Elena? To make me pay? To make me suffer? Is that what you want?"

He's angry, but I can also see a gleam of pain in his eyes.

"Matthew, I..."

I don't know what to say. I'm torn between my anger and my desire to explain to him, to tell him how much his actions have hurt me.

"You don't even know what you want. You're playing a dangerous game, Elena. Stop it right now."

He lets go of me abruptly, and I feel an emptiness, a lack, where his hand used to be.

"It's all your fault."

"My fault? You've got to be kidding me."

The tension is at its peak. I don't even know if I want to slap his perfect cheeks, or kiss his mouth, right here, right now, with all the ardor in me.

"Ray? Seriously, Ray? You couldn't think of a better way to mess with my head? It's completely stupid to behave like that. Besides, now I think he suspects something. Were you born stupid or did it happen afterwards?"

I rage and pull away from his grip. It's amazing the power he has to enrage me in a matter of seconds.

"Leave me alone. You know what I'm gonna do? I'm going to ask for a transfer to Ray's department. It'll be a nice change to get you off my back and have a nicer boss."

"If you do this..."

He doesn't finish his sentence. Instead of finishing, he turns on his heels.

"What, huh?" I stammer.

But he's already gone, melting into the crowd at the bar. I stand there alone, my coat in my hand, my heart beating wildly.

What was that all about? A game of jealousy, a clash of egos? Or something deeper?

I suddenly feel tired, exhausted by the emotion and confusion of the evening. I put on my coat and leave the bar, leaving behind the music, the dancing and an angry Matthew.

Damn, I'm really good at screwing things up.

The night is cool, and I walk slowly home.

Tonight, I may have lost more than I thought. I may have lost a chance to clarify things with Matthew, to understand what's going on between us.

But maybe it's for the best. Maybe distance is what we both need right now.

13

Matthew

To say I'm enraged would be an understatement. Elena is still there, hanging around in my aisle. We haven't said a word to each other all day, even though we're supposed to be working on preparations for this 'special' day at the bookstore. Worst of all, at break time, I saw them flirting again. Usually, Ray never comes to mingle with the other employees. He considers us slaves at best. The last thing he wants is to be seen with us. But the bastard obviously has no limits when it comes to women.

It's a stupid internal war going on between Elena and me. The two of them are staring at each other in the break room. She laughs at all his jokes, no matter how rotten they are. She eats with him. She runs her hand through her hair and...

God, she's beautiful.

I look away, clenching my fists. It's not like me to let jealousy get the better of me, but I can't help it. I'm torn between the desire to join them, to get her out of there, and the awareness that I have to keep my distance for both our sakes.

I return to my work, concentrating on the tasks at hand, but my mind is elsewhere. Every time I hear her laugh, it pierces my heart.

As she returns to the aisle, after spending some time with

Ray, I intercept her.

"What the hell are you doing?"

Elena sighs.

"What? You're going to tell me again that I shouldn't hang out with him."

"Firstly: yes. Secondly, you're supposed to be working."

"Just talking to you makes me want to change departments."

"Well, go on then, do it! What's stopping you, eh?"

"Why do you always have to be such an asshole to me?"

God, she pisses me off! Why does she have so much power over me? It's just not right. She shouldn't be able to get me off track like that, and yet... Every time she talks to me like that, I'm at my wit's end and don't know how to react. Our attraction is magnetic.

"I... I don't know, Elena. I don't want to give you a hard time, but..."

I pause, realizing how confused and lost I am. I hate the idea that she thinks I want to harm her. It's just the opposite. I want to protect her, but from myself first.

"...But what, Matthew?" she asks, her eyes shining with indefinable emotion.

I bite my lip, searching for the right words. I can see she's wavering between anger and sadness.

"I don't want you to get hurt, not by me, not by Ray, not by anyone. I don't know how to explain it to you, but..."

I stop, unable to finish my sentence. I feel that anything I might say would only make things worse.

Elena looks at me, confusion and frustration clearly visible on her face. She shakes her head in exasperation.

"Matthew, I don't understand. One day you're here, the next you're gone. You push me away, then you come back. It's exhausting."

Her voice trembles slightly, and I realize how much I've affected her.

Between us, it's like that. It's...electric. I can almost feel the current. Literally.

She turns on her heel and goes back to work without another word.

Fuck... it's not possible, we'll never make it.

The next thing I know, Ray's nose is between the shelves, beckoning me to join him.

What does this one want?...

This day is going really badly. Very bad.

"In my office," he says laconically.

We walk through the door to his office, then Ray sits down without inviting me to do the same.

"You know why you're here, right?"

"No."

Ray gives me a mocking yet stern look. I don't like his twisted look at all. I've never liked him, but now I hate him even more. Whether at family barbecues or at work, he's unbearable no matter what.

"Elena. You're going to stop hanging around her."

My blood runs cold.

"Why do you care, Ray? That's my private life. It's none of your business."

"Oh, that's my business. You know very well that everything that happens here interests me. And I don't like the way you treat Elena. It's affecting her work."

What a hypocrite.

"What about you? You think your constant advances don't affect her? You're a hypocrite and an asshole."

He rises from his chair, leaning on his desk, coming dangerously close to me.

"I knew it! I knew you were all over her. You see the state

you get in when I mention her name?"

I shudder with anger. Ray, with his superior air and smirk, pushes my buttons.

"I'm not going to let someone like you tell me what to do, especially not about Elena."

Ray leans in even closer.

"This is your last warning, Matthew. Don't push me to take more drastic measures. I could... I don't know... decide to transfer her, for example."

"Just do it. I don't care."

"Well... I see... I could also... tell Betty that you have a new girlfriend and that she works here. Oh, can you imagine how hard life would be for both of you?"

I grit my teeth. That dirty son of a... He's got me and he knows it. The smug, self-satisfied smile he gives me is worth all the jabs in the world. I hate him. I'd throw my fist in his face right now, but he's not even worth getting my knuckles dirty.

"Listen to me, asshole," I squeak. "Do what you want with me, but don't touch Elena. It's out of the question, or else..."

"Or else what?"

"Otherwise, I'll break your face. Your mother, whom I know well, by the way, won't know your face from your ass. Is that enough for you?"

Ray bursts out laughing.

"Are you threatening your superior? You know I can fire you for that?"

"Go ahead, Ray, do it. This goddamn bookstore wouldn't stand without my work. Why don't you go tell Betty you're firing me? We'll see what she thinks."

This time, it's his turn to pull a face. He knows I'm right. He's not the guy to turn this place around. It's my turn to smirk.

"So what, Ray? You're not going to carry out your threat?

Please go ahead, what are you waiting for? Betty would even give me a raise if I asked her, just for the pleasure of having me stay here. Remember, your sister's the boss. You're not."

Ray stares at me, his smile slowly fading as he measures the magnitude of my words. He realizes that I'm not just another employee he can threaten at will. I'm a crucial part of this company, and he knows it.

"You're such a little prick, Matthew," he finally spits. "But I'll be watching you. And if you make the slightest false move, I'll be there to make you pay."

"Watch me all you want. I'm not going to be intimidated by you."

He rises abruptly, the chair creaking under his weight. I stand up straight, ready to face any further threat he might make.

"Now get out of my office. And remember what I told you."

I leave the room without a word, my head held high. On my way out, I pass Elena, who looks at me with a mixture of concern and questioning.

"You and I need to talk," I say.

She frowns. I'm still a little tense from my altercation with Ray.

"What's going on?"

I beckon her to follow me into a quiet corner. We go to the philosophy aisle. At least we won't be disturbed there.

"Are you going to tell me what's going on?"

I shush her by putting my hand over her mouth and she doesn't react. I look left and right to make sure no one is watching us.

"It's about Ray," I murmur. "He knows."

Elena shudders under my hand, her eyes widening. I withdraw my hand, but remain close to her, feeling the electric tension between us.

"What does he know?" she whispers, her voice trembling slightly.

"Everything. About us. He wants to use this to manipulate us, to manipulate *me.*"

She swallows hard, her gaze locked on mine.

"What do you mean?"

"He's threatening to transfer you or talk to Betty. It's very risky for us, Elena."

She instinctively moves closer, seeking comfort. I feel her breath on my skin, and it makes me shiver. I want to protect her, to keep her close to me, but I also know that's not an option. Not if we want to keep our respective jobs. Not if I want to pursue my dream and get the hell out of here with my van. I still need this job. And I suppose she does too.

"What are you going to do?"

I run a hand through my hair in frustration.

"I don't know yet. But I promise, I won't let you down."

Elena raises a hand, hesitantly, then places it on my chest. Her touch is light, but it sends waves of warmth through my whole body. I lean towards her, our proximity intensifying the tension around us.

"Matthew, I..."

Her voice breaks, and I see the emotion in her eyes. I barely restrain myself from taking her in my arms, from kissing her. But I know it's too risky here, now.

"We have to put an end to all this."

She nods, her eyes still fixed on mine. Even though she's just nodded, her gaze says no.

"I know, but it's hard, you know... seeing you every day and not..."

She doesn't finish her sentence, but she doesn't have to. I feel the same way.

"Don't say a word."

"But why can't we just be together?" she asks.

"It would be... too complicated."

She shakes her head angrily.

"You always say that, but the truth is, you're just scared."

"Scared?"

"Yes. About Betty and what people here will think."

She doesn't understand. She doesn't know that if I'm like this, it's only for her own good.

"Don't add to it. It's hard enough as it is."

Elena crosses her arms against her chest, then looks at me sternly.

"In that case, you won't mind if I go out with whoever I want."

"Stop it. This is anything but a game!"

It's not just my career that's at stake, but also my future. My freedom, even. If I get caught up in this, I'll find myself chained by Betty again, and I'll be her lapdog. As for her, she'll find herself without a job, without a penny, and that's not what she deserves, especially since she's just arrived in town.

"If I want to date Ray, I'll date Ray. You don't have to forbid me. Just so we're clear."

Her retort hits me hard, irritating me even more.

"I didn't say I wanted to stop you from seeing whoever you want, Elena. But you have to understand that Ray's only doing this to piss me off and manipulate you."

She clenches her fists, tears of anger in her eyes.

"So what, I'm just a puppet in your little power play? I'm not interesting enough to be flirted with simply for what I am?"

"That's not what I'm saying. I just want you to be safe, that's all."

"And if being with Ray satisfies me, what's it to you?"

These words hit me like a punch. I feel a sharp pain in my chest, mixed with jealousy.

"You can't be serious, Elena. The guy's an asshole! And... you know very well how I feel about you."

Did I really say that out loud?

She seems surprised for a moment, then stares at me, determination in her eyes. I look away, uncomfortable.

"No, I don't. And you don't do anything with those feelings. You hide behind your fears and excuses. I'm tired of waiting for you to make a decision. My life doesn't stop with you."

I approach, frustration bubbling up inside me.

"You want me to make a decision? Very well, then. Ray or me, Elena. You have to choose."

"You have no right to ask this of me, Matthew! I'm not some toy you can just claim whenever you feel like it. You don't own me!"

I'm out of breath, the anger overwhelming me. She's right, I don't have the right to force her to choose, but I can't bear to see her fooling around with Ray.

"So I guess you're going to live up to his expectations, huh? Like nothing between us ever mattered?"

"Perhaps, yes."

She turns to leave, but I hold her by the arm.

"Elena, wait..."

She turns abruptly, wrenching her arm from my grasp.

"Let me go, Matthew. I need time to think."

I watch her go, my heart heavy with regret. I've pushed things too far, and now I risk losing her for good.

14

Elena

Tightening the links in the company, she says, Betty! I feel like I'm spending my evenings on this job!

It's incredible, though. Betty decided to do a kind of 'team-work'. And then she added a bunch of words like 'brainstorming, start-up style, and team building'. In short, terms that sound like they came straight out of a bitch's mouth.

Gee, I shouldn't talk about her like that.

She hasn't done anything to me, I know that, but she's the reason I can't have Matthew and why this whole situation is so... complex.

I sigh, looking at myself in my bedroom mirror. Tonight, I'm out again with my colleagues from the bookstore. One more opportunity for Betty to show that she's the boss. But for me, it's another chance to see Matthew outside our workplace, where we've been avoiding each other for over a week.

I chose a black dress, tight-fitting and slightly plunging at the neckline. Sexy without being too ostentatious. I add a pair of high heels to lengthen my legs. I spend a moment putting on my make-up, emphasizing my eyes and lips. I want him to notice me. I want his gaze to linger on me. I want him to care.

Because yes, I still haven't decided whether to run away from him like the plague, or fight to be with him...

When I look in the mirror, I feel both powerful and vulnerable. Powerful, because I think I'm beautiful and I know I can attract attention. Vulnerable, because a large part of me hopes he'll see more in me than the image I project.

I shake my head, trying to banish these thoughts. Tonight, I'm going to have fun. I'm going to laugh, I'm going to dance. Maybe I'll flirt with other men. I'm going to show Matthew, and myself, that I'm not just some clueless girl. That I'm strong. That I can have a good evening without constantly thinking about him. And that I'm capable of moving on.

I take a deep breath, grab my purse and leave my room. Tonight, Elena is out, and she's going to shine. When Kate sees me arrive, she won't believe her eyes!

But strangely enough, I have a feeling that everything is going to go wrong and there's nothing I can do about it.

As planned, I meet Kate downstairs. She's already waiting for me in her car and when she picks me up, she whistles like a cartoon character.

"Wow, who replaced my friend with an atomic bomb, huh?"

I'm glad she said that. It shows that it works!

"You're all dressed up," she says as I sit in the passenger seat.

"I figured it was a special occasion."

"To make another pass at one of your two suitors? You're spoiled for choice."

I haven't gone back over the discussion we had the other night in the bar about Ray. But I do know that Kate hasn't changed her mind about it. She thinks it's a bad idea and... basically, she's right. But now that things have gotten even murkier with Matthew, I'm not sure of anything. So, I might as well go for it!

Okay, I have feelings. Honestly, they came very prematurely, and I didn't expect to fall under his magnetic spell at all, but... shit, I've got to curb them, repress them, kill them. I can't afford to fall into his trap like that. Anyway, he doesn't know what he wants any more than I do. And even though he's half-confessed to me that he feels something, I get the impression that he only sees me as a girl to hang on his chalkboard for as long as possible, and all to piss Ray McGee off.

"Please don't say that. It's... it's embarrassing."

As she drives, Kate nudges me.

"Come on, admit that you like it deep down."

Well, she's not entirely wrong. But I still have to decide which one I want. Well... Let's be honest... Mathew still occupies all my thoughts, and my heart skips a beat every time I see him. The mere idea of going to this party and seeing him... It makes me really nervous.

I hate this!

But I also know that he'll have to contend with Betty and that I won't have an angle of attack.

"It's not about liking, Kate. It's complicated, you know."

Kate looks at me with a mixture of compassion and malice.

"Elena, it's always complicated with guys. But you're not going to let that spoil your evening, are you? You're beautiful tonight, you should enjoy it."

I sigh, knowing she's right. I can't let Matthew and this whole situation obsess me.

What the...

"I guess you're right. Tonight, I'm going to have fun. And who knows, maybe I'll meet someone interesting."

"Exactly!" exclaims Kate. "And if Matthew sees what he's missing, good for you. But if you taste Ray too, you can tell me which is the best..."

I elbow her back and she bursts out laughing.

"Hey! Don't do that, you cod, I'm driving! You want us to crash?" she shouts.

"Maybe so, if you keep saying stupid things like that."

"Honestly, don't worry about it. Choose who you like best and that's that! It doesn't matter if it's one of them, or someone else."

I smile, but deep down I know that Matthew is on my mind, no matter how hard I try to deny it.

We arrive at the party, and I feel my heart beating a little faster. Music blares from the room, promising a lively night.

"Are you ready for a wild evening?" asks Kate as she pulls over.

"As ready as I can be," I retort, adjusting my dress.

We get out of the car to face our colleagues.

No matter what happens, I promised myself I wouldn't let Matthew spoil my fun. Tonight, I'm Elena, free and bold!

We enter the room where the evening is already in full swing. Colored lights dance on the walls, music blares, people laugh and chat. I let myself be carried away by the atmosphere, determined to distract myself, to free myself from Matthew's grip, at least for a few hours.

Kate and I make our way through the crowd, smiling and ready to enjoy. I feel eyes on me, some admiring, others curious.

Suddenly, I see *him* standing by the bar, talking to some colleagues. Our eyes meet, and a spark of electricity crosses the space between us. I quickly look away, remembering my promise not to let him affect me.

"Shall we dance?" suggests Kate, pulling me towards the dance floor.

I nod and we join in. The music envelops my senses, and I let myself go with the rhythm, forgetting everything else. Tension, frustration - all evaporate in the energy I put into my movements.

It's a great place to spend an evening and forget your troubles. For the occasion, Betty has had the place privatized – and she hasn't even arrived yet. No doubt a way for her to show that she's the richest and most powerful. I'm not naive; I know it's not just a matter of kindness and a desire to please her employees. Betty wants to rise above us. It's also a well-played game of influence.

Rah, I hate myself for being so jealous of her. I shouldn't be.

As I brood over my thoughts, the crowd suddenly stirs, drawing my attention to the entrance. Betty has just arrived. She's absolutely impeccable, dressed in an elegant gown that accentuates her figure, her hair perfectly coifed, a confident smile on her lips. She exudes an aura of power and control that leaves no one indifferent. Even Kate is speechless.

I can't help watching her as she greets some of her employees, her smile never losing its sparkle. She has this gift for being the center of attention, for captivating her audience. It's both fascinating and frightening. And always with those damned big eyes that seem to pierce you like daggers.

Kate and I are posed at counter level, our glasses in hand.

Betty approaches the bar, ordering a drink with natural confidence. She seems totally at ease, as if she was born to be in the spotlight, to lead and influence all these people.

I suddenly feel small and insignificant next to her. She has everything I don't: confidence, power, influence. And above all, she has a hold over Matthew, something I can neither understand nor fight.

When her eyes meet mine, I'm confused. I feel like she's angry with me. That she's looking at me with an inquisitive look.

I quickly look away, concentrating on my own drink. This is supposed to be a relaxing evening, but Betty's presence turns it into a show of force. I wonder how Matthew is handling all this, how he feels about this woman who seems to control everything around her, even though they've broken up.

And suddenly, the worst happens. Just as I'm trying to make myself forget - preferably for good - Betty speaks to me.

"Elena. Nice dress."

My heart is beating a mile a minute.

Shit, shit, shit...Why is she talking to me?

"Thank you."

Betty laughs loudly, then puts a hand on my shoulder.

"Don't worry, we're not at work. You can relax."

It's funny, but when she says that, I feel anything but relaxed. Quite the opposite, in fact.

"Are you trying to please someone in particular?"

His gaze lingers on my dress, my make-up, in short, my outfit as a whole, and I feel as if his eyes are piercing through my soul.

"What? What an idea! No, no..."

Fuck, she must suspect something. I'm toast. We're toast. We're screwed. Betty's gonna kill us, then necromantically resurrect us, then kill us again.

At the same time, maybe her brother told her about me... After all, it's not as if we went unnoticed in the bookstore, chatting so often together.

"Too bad," she says, grabbing her glass to dip her lips in it. "I thought Ray had finally found someone. Well, I have to warn you: I don't really like people hanging around my brother, but... that's his choice, isn't it? I just wanted to make sure you were a good girl. But I guess you are, aren't you?"

Too much information at once. I don't know what to say.

"Uh... yes, yes, of course, I..."

Betty stares at me with a smile that's meant to be reassuring, but only accentuates my unease.

A little more and I can see a canine gleam between his lips.

"I'm glad to hear it. You know, Elena, I'm very concerned

about my brother and his well-being. The same goes for my employees."

I nod, trying to sound convinced. Betty seems to read me like an open book. Her intuition is almost frightening.

"That's nice. Enjoy the evening," she adds, before wandering off to another group.

I stand there frozen, trying to regain my composure. Meeting Betty was more intense than I could have imagined. Her presence, her charisma, the way she controls conversation... it's all... intimidating.

I head for a quieter corner of the room, looking for some respite. As I walk, my eyes meet those of Matthew. He stares at me with an indecipherable expression. I don't know what he's thinking, what he's feeling. Everything is so complicated with him, so full of unspoken emotions.

I lean against a wall, taking a deep breath. It's going to be a long and challenging evening. Betty, Matthew, Ray... Everyone seems to be advancing their pawns, and I feel trapped between their ambitions and desires. And then there's Kate, who doesn't give a damn and is circling Travis like a wasp around a merguez sausage.

God, sometimes I wish I could be like her...

She doesn't care about all that, Kate. Does she want to? She takes. It's as simple as that. Me, I twist my mind all over the place trying not to offend anyone's sensibilities - too much. But the truth is, most of the time, I get stepped on, even if I try to be a bit of a rebel - my character's to blame.

I close my eyes for a moment, trying to refocus, when Ray arrives at my level with an enticing smile. He looks a little drunk. Obviously, he started the evening before we did - along with a few other colleagues who are downright soaked as sponges. Maybe he can hold his liquor better.

"Hi, Elena. Are you having a good time?"

His smile is charming, but I sense a certain insistence be-hind his words, as if he wants something from me.

"Yes," I retort with a hint of reluctance.

"I noticed you seemed a bit tense. I thought a little compa-ny might loosen you up," he says, moving slightly closer.

I take a step back, uncomfortable. Ray is attractive, sure, but there's something about his attitude tonight that makes me uneasy. Maybe the fact that he's so close to Betty, and I don't want to get further entangled with my boss's family, is misleading me? Or maybe... the fact that he smells of alcohol? Or... that he has that unhealthy spark of desire in his eyes? I feel like a lecherous object in his eyes.

Burp...

"Thank you, Ray, but I'm fine. I just need some air."

"Come on, Elena... We're here to have fun, after all. My company wouldn't do you any harm! Besides, I find you really attractive tonight. You're downright... sexy!"

His voice is suave, almost too much so. He puts his hand on my arm and I shiver, not with pleasure, but with apprehension.

"Ray, I really like you as a colleague, but I don't think this is a good idea," I say, trying to put some distance between us.

Right now, I'm in a really tense situation. If I reject him, I'll hear about it, and on the other hand, I don't really like him sticking to me like that.

Ray's pressure becomes more and more obvious, and I feel my unease growing. He doesn't seem to understand my refus-al, or worse, he chooses to ignore it.

"Don't play coy," he insists, drawing even closer. "You look beautiful tonight, and I'm sure we could have a lot of fun to-gether. You didn't put on that dress just to dance, did you?"

I try to pull away, but he tightens his grip on my arm. His attitude is no longer simply insinuating, it's downright inva-sive.

"Ray, let go of me, I'm not interested," I let go firmly, trying to keep my composure.

He smiles, a smile that is anything but reassuring.

"But come on... We're just colleagues, there's nothing wrong with that, is there?" he pleads.

I feel trapped, unable to escape without creating an incident. I look around for a way out, for someone to help me, but the crowd seems oblivious to the tension between Ray and me. Kate is clinging to Travis, and no one seems to be paying any attention to us.

"Ray, I'm serious. Stop it right now" I thunder, my voice trembling.

"Come on, let's take a look around."

Without leaving me any other choice, his hand becomes a pair of handcuffs and he forcefully leads me into a darker corner. I know exactly what he has in mind and I feel helpless. His fingers are hurting me now, and his lustful gaze shines with appetite.

I feel like throwing up.

"Let me go..."

"I've been thinking about you all week, you know? Don't be so defensive."

"I think she asked you to let her go," thunders a familiar voice.

Matthew.

I've rarely been so happy to see him.

"Well, well, well... the knight in shining armor who turns up. Are you forgetting what I told you the other day in my office?"

I know how much he's putting himself at risk for my sake. If he openly defends me, he also exposes himself to Betty's wrath.

The tension rises a notch when Matthew steps between us, forcing him to loosen his grip on me. There's anger in his eyes, like never before. Ray, for his part, straightens up, his expression changing from surprise to a provocative smile.

"Ah, Matthew, always the hero," he sneers. "But what happens between Elena and me is none of your business."

Matthew stands in front of me, his body taut as a crossbow ready to be unleashed. I can feel he's about to crack, and I'm afraid the situation is about to get out of hand.

"Leave her alone, Ray," Matthew scolds. "She told you no. That's pretty clear, I think."

"Oh, you care what she might want now?" replies Ray scornfully. "Since when?"

"Since..."

Matthew doesn't finish his sentence.

"Ever since you've been in love with her?" he asks wryly. "Or what is it? Is it because you don't want us to touch your toys?"

"Elena is anything but a toy, you bastard."

I have a feeling this isn't going to end well.

It CAN'T end well.

Tempers flare, words fly, and before I can intervene, the situation explodes. Ray pushes Matthew, who immediately retaliates. They come to blows, pushing and shoving each other. The situation is chaotic, and the other guests begin to gather around them.

It's all my fault. God, what a mess... I've started a boxing match!

I'm trying to take a deep breath, remembering that they were already rivals before I arrived, but, let's be honest, I haven't helped matters at all.

All the guests now seem to be getting closer.

"Leave her alone," Matthew spits.

"She's not yours!" exclaims Ray.

OK, as if the situation wasn't clear enough for everyone; now it's much more explicit. Great...

15

Elena

Thunder rumbles in the bar. Luckily, it's been privatized for the occasion. In their fight, Ray and Matthew look like two wild animals, trying to assert their dominance. In Ray's case, it's ridiculous. In Matthew's case... I admit it's sexy. But I'm not impartial. It's seeing him flex his muscles like that. It's... quite unsettling. Ray may be well built, but he doesn't stand a chance against Matthew. I know exactly what's under his clothes and... it's solid. Almost reinforced concrete.

"What the hell have you done?" asks Kate, rushing over to try and separate them.

Travis puts down his glass and steps in too, and only once the two beasts are calmer does Betty appear.

Oh, shit... I feel like I'm going to get the short end of the stick.

"What's going on here?" she thunders.

This is it. The return of the bossy woman who doesn't let anything get past her. I wasn't looking forward to meeting her again.

"Oh, Betty... I'm glad you're here," Ray says, holding his nose. "Just one more thing with that jerk of an ex-boyfriend of yours, you know."

She turns to Matthew, who wipes his lip with a curt gesture. His fight had left a small mark on him, but nothing like what Ray has suffered. It's true that Matthew didn't pull any punches when he landed a right hook. I thought his nostrils were going to fall out, roll under a table and he'd never be able to pick them up.

"You two, I'm getting sick of your bullshit. But until now, you've never come to blows. So, what happened?"

"It's good you asked," retorts Ray. "I think Matthew has something to tell you. Don't you, Matthew?"

Oh, no... He's not going to do that...

Suddenly, the story of the last few weeks flashes through my mind and my heart races. I feel on the verge of emptiness.

The tension in the air is electric. Betty stares at Matthew with an intensity that could pierce anyone. Ray, despite his air of defiance, seems a little more uncertain, but he doesn't waste the opportunity to put Matthew in an awkward position. The latter is calm on the surface, but I can see the storm raging in his eyes.

There's a moment of silence, a silence heavy with expectation.

"I have nothing to say, Betty," Matthew finally replies in a firm voice. "This is between Ray and me."

Betty frowns, clearly displeased with the answer. She looks around, her gaze lingering briefly on me, and I can feel my heart pounding in my throat. I wonder if she's guessed something about Matthew and me.

"It's unacceptable, in any case," she declares in an icy voice. "I don't like being kept in the dark about anything, and you know it. So, I'll ask Ray instead..."

★ ★ ★

162

Matthew

I don't want Elena to suffer, but on the other hand, right now, I'm up against the wall. When I see that asshole's satisfied smile, I know exactly what he's going to say.

"I'm just defending my sister's honor, and I think that's only fair, don't you?" claims Ray.

That dirty little bastard.

I know exactly where he's going with this and I have a feeling I'm not going to like it at all.

"Ray..." I squeak.

"What's the matter, big boy? Don't you want me to tell everyone your little secret? Well, I think the others have a right to know, don't you?"

"You have no idea what you're talking about. The truth is that your brother, Betty, was forcing Elena to do things she hadn't consented to," I finally blurt out.

And inevitably, Ray drapes himself in his bad faith, playing the offended.

"What are you talking about? Elena and I were just having fun. I don't know what you're talking about."

He glances coldly at Elena, who immediately understands that her job is at stake if she says anything. So, she bows her head. It looks like I'll have to handle this one on my own. She doesn't have the courage to take sides. I know she cares too much about her job at the bookstore. As a result, I screwed myself with my intervention. Now I'm going to have to find an explanation for all this.

"Ray, you know very well what you were doing, and it wasn't 'just having fun'", I retort, my voice betraying some of my frustration. 'Fun' was the last thing on your mind."

Betty looks at Ray, then at me, her expression oscillating between disbelief and suspicion. Ray, for his part, tries to maintain his innocent air, but I can see he's beginning to lose his confidence.

"I think you're exaggerating," he says in a slightly less confident voice. "It was just a joke."

I shake my head in exasperation. I turn to Betty.

"Betty, I assure you, it wasn't a joke. It was much more serious than that."

"Let's talk about your relationship with Elena," my opponent suggests.

My blood runs cold. This time, I'm screwed. Betty's eyes widen and I realize I'm going to have to do some serious explaining.

"No, because Matthew says a lot of things, but he doesn't prove anything. Elena has nothing to reproach me for. Isn't that true?"

Again, she remains silent.

Hello bravery.

On the other hand, she's probably in shock and I find myself alone in this arena, caught in the crossfire between Ray and Betty. I'll have to face the dragons without any help.

"So, if Elena has nothing to reproach Ray for, why did you start hitting him?"

And that's it. The trap closes and I'm caught between its sharp jaws.

"Because he's in love with her," says Ray.

I make big eyes. I want to hit him again. I'm furious. Not only is he screwing me personally, but he's also screwing Elena, and that's worse than anything. I can't accept it, because it would be my fault.

"Stop talking bullshit," I retort, clenching my jaw.

"You're not? Well, you're attracted to her, then."

Worst of all, he keeps talking. And as he spouts his bullshit, Betty shows signs of anger. I can see it in her eyes. I know her well enough to know when it's coming. Of course, she tries to remain dignified and the signs are imperceptible to anyone who doesn't know her. But I've lived with her long enough to know what it's like. And the worst thing about her is the anger. Because she never thunders like a storm raging against everything around her. No. It's cold anger. Calculated. Even more brittle. It's a thousand times crueler and deadlier than someone who lets their emotions explode. Betty holds them in, represses them, and under a facade of controlled propriety, she delivers razor-sharp words.

"Really?" she asks.

I glance at Elena. She's decomposing.

Damn it, I can't lose this job. I can't lose it now. I just can't.

If I give up the bookstore, I'm also giving up my dream, and I can't allow that. I need to escape and live life on my own terms. I only had a few months to go before everything was settled, and this could precipitate things and make them terribly dangerous for my future. I'd have a hard time finding such a well-paid job, and that would put off my project for quite some time.

I can't get involved in this.

"Betty, I assure you it's not what you think," I say, trying to remain calm.

Betty stares at me with an intensity that would make anyone cringe. She seems to be weighing up every word I say, trying to sort out the true from the false.

"Elena, I'd like to hear from you," she says, turning to her.

Elena looks up, visibly hesitant. I can see she's struggling with herself, not knowing what to say.

"Betty, I'm... I'm just a little lost in all this," she begins hesitantly. "Ray... he was a little too insistent, but I don't think he had any bad intentions."

I feel a twinge of sadness at her words. I understand that she's trying to save her job, too, but it also means that I've been left out of the story.

Betty seems satisfied with this answer and turns back to me.

"Well... looks like you're the only problem here, Matthew."

I'm boiling inside. I mustn't explode. I mustn't let my anger out.

I decide to go for it and bluff.

"Are you serious? I'm this close to quitting right now."

"Quitting? Why should you? Did I say you were the only problem? Mmh... I guess I was a little wrong about that."

Betty looks at Elena and, immediately, I understand.

No. Not that.

"Did something happen between you?" continues Betty.

Elena couldn't think of anything to say. She stammers shyly.

So, it's Ray who takes the floor again, to hammer home the point.

"I've already caught them making out in the storeroom. I told Matthew it wasn't right. Especially to you. But he wouldn't listen. You know how he is."

So in the end, the day he surprised us, he knew what was going on. So, the fact that he got closer to Elena is purely calculated. He's deliberately trying to get in my way.

What an asshole!

"Tell me, Matthew... is it true?"

Elena is nothing but a puddle on the ground.

"No, it isn't. None of this is true."

I glance at my companion and, once again, she seems to be decomposing.

166

"You're a liar. You were sweating sex!"

Elena finally raises her eyes to mine and looks at me.

"Please," she begs. "Tell the truth…"

"Is all this true?" insists Betty. "Matthew?"

If I say yes, I fault myself. If I say no, I put Elena at fault. She'll look like a seductress and a liar. She's just arrived. Nobody knows her…

I'm sorry for her, but… I can't. I can't afford to lose my job. Not when I'm so close.

"No," I say.

"That's enough! This time it's too much."

She seems to be losing her patience. This is not a good sign. Her jealousy is overriding the inordinate control she's trying to exert over herself. I think a big storm is coming. The last time she was this out of control was when we split up. It was a series of screams and tears on her part. I thought she was going to suffocate, asphyxiate and die. Thinking about it now, and knowing her, it must have been an act. Still, I felt guilty about putting her through it.

But I still managed to extricate myself from its clutches.

"Elena, you can already consider yourself fired. For serious misconduct. You're a seductress and a liar. I don't want that on my team. We're all about positive management and a positive attitude, whatever the circumstances. If you cause trouble, you're not welcome," she declares coldly.

The principal concerned breaks down inwardly. I can see it in her eyes.

"What? But…" she stammers.

"You can go. You can go now."

Betty's tone is unmistakable.

Without another word, Elena goes to the check-room to grab her jacket. Tears well up in her eyes, and before she's even left the bar, grief has already stained her cheeks.

It's all my fault.

I stand there, petrified, watching Elena make her way towards the exit before the eyes of our stunned colleagues. My heart sinks. I know I've made the most cowardly decision. I sacrificed Elena to save my own skin. Guilt gnaws at my insides, but it's already too late.

I turn to Betty, searching for words to explain or perhaps to defend myself, but nothing comes out. She fixes me with an icy stare.

"Matthew, I'm disappointed. I thought you were better than this," she says sharply.

I lower my head, unable to meet his gaze. I feel tiny, crushed under the weight of my own choices. No matter how many times I tell myself that she no longer has any control over me, when she looks at me like that, I can still feel the embrace of the leash she once slipped around my neck.

"I'm sorry, Betty. But you didn't have to do this. We're not together anymore. Elena didn't do anything wrong."

"It's not enough. She doesn't deserve to stay with us. I don't want any trouble and too bad for the event. You're on your own. You'll have to prove to me that you deserve your place here. Right now, I'm not convinced."

"I suppose you'd rather I left?"

"You think I don't know you're dying for it? But on the other hand... you need the money, don't you? The roles are reversed. I've got the power over you, Matthew. Don't forget it," she says in a more measured voice, so that only I can hear.

Forced to swallow my pride, I nod, knowing I'll have to work twice as hard to regain his trust, and maybe even some semblance of respect from my colleagues.

Eventually, they scatter, murmuring, and the evening returns to normal, as if nothing had happened. I'm elsewhere. My mind is with Elena, who left in tears because of me. I should have been honest. I should have taken responsibility for our actions. Instead, I took the easy way out. I chose my own safety when I wanted to protect her, and now I have to live with the consequences.

I watch Betty walk away to talk to other guests, then quietly slip away from the party. I need some air, need to think about everything that's just happened.

As I head for the exit, someone calls out to me.

"Proud of yourself, I hope?"

Kate.

I don't usually hang out with her. Or not very much. I understood that she was Elena's best friend.

"If you're here for the blame, don't bother. I'm already flogging myself."

"You can, yeah, buddy. Because Elena, you see, she really loved her job! And she liked you, too. Now you've just thrown it all away to save yourself. She'll have a hard time finding another job, and I wouldn't be surprised if she has to leave again."

Great, I needed the best friend's reproach.

"Shame on you, Matthew. Elena didn't deserve this, she's innocent in all this," she spits with palpable anger.

I bow my head, knowing she's right. I've acted selfishly, thinking only of my own situation without considering Elena's.

I have to make it up to you.

"I know, I know I did wrong, but I couldn't afford to lose my job," I murmur.

"Great," she says. "You get to keep your job. And lose all the respect of your colleagues. As for her, she'll have to pack again."

Cold as ice, she finally turns on her heels and disappears.

All around me, every laugh, every animated conversation painfully reminds me of Elena's absence and the seriousness of my actions. I prefer to leave the premises as quickly as possible and slip into the darkness of the street without a sound.

I return home, winding my way through the dark, silent streets. Each step reminds me of the growing distance between Elena and me. When I arrive home, the apartment feels strangely empty and cold. I sit on the sofa in the dark, my thoughts in a jumble.

I hate myself.

I think back to everything that happened, to every moment shared with Elena, to our laughter, our conversations, our intimate moments. And how I ruined it all out of fear and cowardice. The images of the evening come back to me, the distress in Elena's eyes, the anger in Betty's, Kate's reproaches.

I realize the extent of my fault. I should have been honest, I should have faced up to the consequences of my actions. But instead, I let my fear dictate my actions, and now I'm alone, racked by remorse and guilt.

The hours tick by slowly, and sleep eludes me. Elena's face imposes itself on my mind, like a final torment.

It's at times like these that I usually need to surf the most. I didn't win anything tonight. Nothing. Not only am I back in Betty's pocket, but Elena has lost her job and I'll probably never hear from her again. I absolutely must make it up to her. Somehow.

Nothing is ever lost. No ?

16

Elena

From the bottom of my bed, I want to cry after what happened. How could Matthew do this to me? All I want now is to leave. To leave San Francisco. I'm as destroyed as I've ever been. I thought I'd change my life by coming here and, in the end, it's worse rather than better.

Thoughts race through my head, each one more painful than the last. The image of Matthew, of his impassive face as he rejected me in front of everyone, haunts me. Tears roll silently down my cheeks, an expression of the pain and betrayal I feel.

I think back to my arrival in San Francisco, full of hope and excitement for a new beginning. I had dreams, ambitions, a desire to discover this city and thrive here. And now, here I am, broken, betrayed by someone I had begun to trust and feel strongly about.

The idea of leaving everything behind, becomes more and more tempting. San Francisco, which represented a new beginning, is now synonymous with pain and disappointment. The city itself seems to remind me of Matthew's betrayal at every street corner, every view of the Golden Gate Bridge.

I feel like everything I've built is crumbling around me. My job, my relationships, my dreams... everything seems to have vanished in an instant, leaving behind an immense void. The disappointment is so deep that it consumes me, preventing me from seeing a way out.

But in the midst of this pain, there's a small voice, a spark of defiance. A refusal to let this ordeal define me, a desire to get back up and prove that I'm stronger than this. I remind myself that I came here to change my life, to live my dreams, and I realize that I can't let one person, one event, break that.

I came here to forget what happened to me back in New York. That disastrous engagement, that painful separation, that boring job. And then, here, there's Kate...

My phone screen lights up.

* *Everything okay, honey?*

* *Not really...*

* *I'm sorry. I'm sorry. I'm sorry. For what happened. Matthew really behaved like a huge asshole!*

* *The king of assholes!*

* *What are you going to do?*

At the moment, I have no idea. I don't really know. I guess I'll take advantage of my new - precarious - situation to take a walk around town and discover my new home for good.

* *I'll think about it...*

* *Try to get some rest. And if you need anything, don't forget I'm here.*

The night is restless. I have a hard time falling asleep and, when I think about this new life, I tell myself that I'll soon have to find a way to support myself. I can't live on love and fresh water. And anyway, when it comes to 'love', I don't think it's for me. There's always fresh water, but it's not very nourishing.

In the morning, I wake up without any help. Only the bitterness of realizing that my body is like clockwork and that I should normally be getting ready for work. The more I think about it, the tighter my heart becomes. I really loved this bookstore. Okay, there were some drawbacks. First, Betty. Then there was my boundless attraction to Matthew and the blunder we both made before we even knew who each other were. But still... I was working among books! I was in my own world, and above all, I was about to finalize the organization of a beautiful literary event that was going to bring together a whole bunch of local authors for a superb evening.

I must forget all that...

Since I've got some free time, I decide to take a stroll around town, just to soak it all in. I absolutely must find something else to do. I'm not one to give up so easily. The urge to leave town has crossed my mind - more than once, since last night - but that would be an admission of failure and I'm not a loser. No. I always fight to get what I want.

I get ready, putting on a casual, comfortable outfit, ideal for a walk. I want to be myself, free and independent, away from the complications of the bookstore and Matthew. And I won't give my parents the satisfaction of showing them that I've failed.

I wander around with no precise destination, letting my steps guide me. I pass lively cafés, inviting bookstores and green parks. The city is lively and dynamic, and I remember why I came here. It wasn't just to escape New York and its painful memories, it was also to discover a new world, to ex-

173

perience new things.

As I walk around, I think about what I really want. I realize that my passion for books is still intact, despite what happened at the bookstore. Maybe I could get a job in another bookstore, or even start something new, something different. Maybe I could even go back to school or take on a project that's close to my heart.

All in all, this could be the start of something new...

Why not write?

It's... what I've been dreaming of all this time, without daring to admit it to myself. I did say it, it's true, but only to Matthew, and I'd told Kate a little about it. I'd told her what I had in mind, and with her usual air of self-assurance she'd said to me: "But go ahead, damn it, what are you waiting for, you codger? Go for it!"

I had this first project, yes, that... I can always go back to. But I need a literary agent for that, and more often than not I get dozens of rejection letters. All the same, I want to get on with it. If only... for myself!

In life, I've never had time for anything. That's just the way it is. First, there was studying. Then there was the boyfriend - fiancé - then the job and now, for the first time, I can finally breathe and take some time for myself. So, instead of seeing it as a nightmare, or a bottomless pit of sadness, I prefer to see it as a form of providence. An opportunity not to be missed. Under any circumstances.

I stop in front of an art and stationery store, attracted by the colorful and inspiring display of notebooks and pens. A shy smile forms on my lips.

Why not?

It's been so long since I've taken the time to write for myself, for the pure pleasure of creation. For too long, I've repressed what I really wanted.

I enter the store, lulled by the soft melody of a bell above the door. The air is filled with the scent of fresh paper and ink, a fragrance that awakens distant memories of evenings spent blacking out pages of my innermost thoughts, my wildest dreams. I've always told myself that it's just a *hobby*, but... a *hobby is just* a hobby, as long as you don't try to go any further.

Maybe it's time for me to go further.

I stroll among the shelves, delicately touching the covers of the notebooks, leafing through them, letting myself be charmed by their texture, their weight. Finally, I choose a notebook with a soft leather cover, in a deep blue, adorned with delicate motifs. It's perfect. It reminds me of this old school notebook I used to have when I was still at school. I used to write my stories in it.

On my way out, I settle down in a quiet corner of town, armed with a black ink pen I've also bought, and start writing. The words flow from my pen with surprising ease. I draw up the outline of my novel, a story that has been brewing in my mind for years, but which I've never had the courage to put down on paper.

I outline the plot, draw the contours of my characters, imagine the twists and turns. Every word, every sentence is a step closer to realizing a dream I thought was out of reach.

As I write, I feel the spark of passion ignite within me. It's an incredible, exhilarating feeling. I'm lost in my own world, a world where I can create, explore and freely express everything I feel, everything I am.

The pen glides across the paper, tracing the stories of characters who gradually become real to me. It's an escape, a refuge, a source of immense joy.

I don't know how much time I spend like this, immersed in my world of ink and paper. When I finally raise my head, I'm surprised to see that the sun has started to set.

When I get up again, I feel invigorated, full of new energy. I have a project, a goal, something that belongs to me and that no one can take away from me. Not even Matthew. I need to channel all this new energy into something more creative.

When I get home, it's almost dark, once I get settled in, there's a knock on my door.

I don't know why, but for a moment, I hope it's Matthew, overcome with remorse, who's come to apologize and tell me everything's okay. My heart is beating a mile a minute, but as soon as I open the door, I come face to face with Kate, a bottle of wine in her hand, and a discomfited look on her face.

"I know you're not feeling too good, so... I brought some wine. What do you think? Is this enough of an offering?"

In truth, not really... but I appreciate the intention.

I let her in, without forcing myself to smile. Even though I didn't work at the bookstore today, it wasn't such a bad day - if we're talking productivity and creativity.

Kate places the bottle on the table in my living room, then gives me a hug.

"I'm sorry, I came as soon as I could, after... well, after the..."

"Work, yes, I know. I get it."

She sighs heavily.

"You know, I can't believe what he did to you," she begins. "Matthew is such a jerk."

I nod, feeling that lump in my throat again. The betrayal and pain are still raw, but I refuse to let them overwhelm me.

"Yes, he is. But you know what? I'm going to be fine. I started writing today," I say, showing her my new notebook.

Her eyes light up.

"Really? That's great, Elena! Are you finally going to write your novel?"

I smile, feeling a thrill of excitement at the idea of sharing this with her.

"Yes, I'm going to do it. And I'm going to give it my all."

We settle on the sofa, and Kate uncorks the bottle of wine. She fills our glasses, and we toast to a better future, to new opportunities.

"To your new chapter," says Kate, raising her glass.

I raise mine in response.

"Here's to a fresh start!"

"So, are you going to become the next best-selling author?"

I almost choke on my wine.

"Honestly, I don't think so. And that's not why I do it. I... I just need to write. That's all it is. It's a great outlet and I've gone too long without it."

"Well... you don't want to know how today went, do you?"

Part of me wants it... part of me doesn't.

"Yes, tell me about it."

Kate takes a sip of wine, then begins to tell me about the day in detail.

"It was... weird without you. Betty tried to act as if nothing had happened, but the mood was tense. Matthew seemed absent, distracted. It was like he was regretting something, well, I don't know. He locked himself in his office and continued with the preparations for the event. At least, that's what he said. And then Betty decided to help him, eventually. So... they spent their time together. Shit, I realize what I'm telling you might not be so great..."

I listen carefully, trying to keep my emotions at bay. The idea that Matthew might feel remorse touches me, but I remind myself that it's too late for that. And then, the pang in my heart comes quickly. Especially when she brings up the fact that Betty is trying to get back at him. I'd rather change the subject.

"And Ray?" I ask.

"Oh, him... He tried to play the victim, but nobody really fell for it. I think people are starting to see his true face."

I nod thoughtfully. It's hard to believe this whole situation happened in such a short time. It was like a whirlwind, an emotional chaos that left me exhausted and lost. Everything changed in the blink of an eye.

"Listen, Elena," Kate begins, placing her hand on my knee. "What matters is that you concentrate on yourself now. Forget Matthew, forget the bookstore. You have incredible talent, and I'm sure you're going to do extraordinary things. Don't you agree?"

I smile at her, grateful for her support.

"Thank you, Kate. I guess you're right. It's time to focus on me and my projects. And you too, right?"

She looks puzzled, as if she doesn't know what I'm talking about. Then I frown, to make her understand.

"Oh, I see... you mean Travis. No, no, it's nothing like that. This is everyday body work. It's not just a... fling, you know? I wish I could move as fast as you with Matthew, but honestly, it's kind of complicated."

I laugh at Kate's comment. It's good to see that she too has her own challenges, her own battles to fight. It reminds me that life goes on, despite setbacks and disappointments.

"You know, Kate, every story is different. Take your time with Travis. It doesn't have to be a race," I say with a wink.

"You're right. But every time I see it, my panties burst into flames. It's getting expensive in the underwear department."

I can't help but burst out laughing at Kate's remark. Her sense of humor is as refreshing as ever, even in the most tense of situations. At least she manages to make me forget the problems of the previous day.

"Well, maybe you should invest in stronger materials," I suggest with a laugh.

She laughs along with me. Here I'm back to the lightness of when we were younger and hadn't yet experienced the setbacks of adult life.

"Do you think they make flame-retardant panties?" she asks me with a falsely serious air.

"If not, it's a business idea you might be interested in," I retort, amused.

We keep laughing and chatting, leaving our worries and cares behind us. It's a breath of fresh air, a much-needed moment of relaxation.

"Seriously, Kate, you have incredible strength. I'm sure things will work out with Travis. You deserve someone extraordinary, and I know you'll find him," I add, sincerely. "If I had to list your qualities, I'd say you're: fun, silly and a little bit of a slut."

"Nah, nah, nah," she corrects me. "Very naughty if it's with Travis. At least as dirty as you were with Matthew."

"Tell me about it..."

Now we're back to a subject that's a little more sensitive and a little less amusing, inevitably. I didn't expect him to have such a hold on me, and yet he does. I have to admit it. I'd so like to see him again...

"Well, in a way, I feel a little guilty too, you know," she admits. "Because, without me, you wouldn't have met him under these conditions. It's kind of because of that Tinder profile I created for you, you know what I mean?"

I don't blame him. Because even though it's all totally chaotic and I'm heartbroken, Matthew has still been one of my greatest stories. A story that, technically, hasn't even started yet.

"You have nothing to feel guilty about. It's not your fault. He's the one who screwed up, with his stories."

"If it makes you feel any better," she continues, waving her

179

hands, "everyone's giving him the cold shoulder. I don't think he'll last long in the bookstore before he bolts."

That's not what I wanted either.

I know why Matthew is still in this business. It's to have enough and realize his dream. Otherwise, he would have quit a long time ago. Even though I'm angry with him, I don't want him to go through hell at work.

"It's not even what I want, you know?"

"You're much too nice. He doesn't deserve your sympathy. Seriously, huh?"

Kate looks genuinely annoyed. She dips her lips in the wine - no doubt a way of calming herself. Her unwavering support makes me very happy. But Matthew's suffering won't bring my job back. All I can do now is concentrate on myself and these new projects I want to accomplish. As for him, well... we'll see.

"And you, you're a real femme fatale and you'll soon have Travis in your net."

She smiles at me, touched by my words.

"Will I be your child's godmother?" I ask, laughing.

"Of course. You betcha! Let's have a serious talk, shall we?"

His air becomes much more serious again.

"I know he hurt you, I know you probably want to slash the tires on his car, but... do you want him back?"

Slashing the Mustang's tires? That would be a real waste.

If I'm honest... I'd at least like to see him again. So that we can explain ourselves, he and I.

"All I want is an explanation. A good tête-à-tête."

"We know how it'd end up," she says, rolling her eyes.

"Not this time. There'd be nothing hot about it. Take my word for it. It would be a stern tête-à-tête of its kind."

But necessary...

17

Matthew

A fortnight passed. No news from Elena. Not a word. I didn't expect a message from her at the same time. Not after what I'd done. But, I don't know, maybe I was waiting for a little sign, or outright a miracle, somehow.

I find myself wandering around my apartment, lost in thought. Each passing day reminds me more and more of the magnitude of my mistake. I let Elena go, chose my career and my project instead of defending her, and now I feel empty, haunted by her absence. Every time I arrive at the bookstore, it's a new stab in my chest, because she's no longer there. Her absence is felt. But then, miracles only happen at Christmas. And even then... If I have to wait for Betty to make a gesture for her, I can wait all my life. She'll never lift a finger. Her sentence is irrevocable. Even the whole of San Francisco, a city of sun, joy, surf and beach, seems to me as gray as the East Coast.

I find myself looking at my phone, still hoping, against hope, for a message from Elena, some proof that she's still thinking about me, that there's still a chance. But the screen remains hopelessly blank.

Sometimes I wonder what she's doing, where she is, if she's found a new job, if she's happy. I wonder if she thinks about me, if she regrets what happened between us as much as I do.

The worst part is the feeling of helplessness, the regret that overwhelms me. I should have been honest from the start, I should have supported her, I should have risked my job for her. But I didn't, and now I'm paying the price for my cowardice.

It's not who I am, damn it... When did I become so selfish? Was it Betty who rubbed off on me like that?

The void his departure has left is deeper than I could have imagined.

Should I try to contact her, apologize, fix what I've broken? But I hold back, afraid of hurting her more. I also know that my ego is still in the balance, and I blame myself for being like this. My past history has damaged me much more than I thought.

Just as I'm going through my little depression, I hear a knock at the door. I don't know why, but I start hoping it's Elena. After all, she knows I live here. Anything's possible.

"Hey, lazy!"

That's Anton's voice. He's probably accompanied by...

I open the door and get confirmation. Derek's here, too.

"What are you doing?" he says.

I must look like shit. Unshaven, tired, dark circles under my eyes and, above all, Elena on my mind. She can't leave my thoughts, it's unbearable.

Without asking my permission, Anton enters, followed by my other friend.

"Please make yourself at home."

"I knew it," says Anton, picking up a book from my sofa. "Poetry. You're moping! I know you... It's Saturday, it's a beautiful day outside and you're reading poetry."

"Lay off the poetry, man. It's not you," says Derek, settling back into my chair. "That's Matthew on a bad day. We're here to get you out of your hole. So, what's going on?"

I sigh, realizing that my friends are right. I've fallen into a spiral of melancholy since Elena left, and they're here to shake me up a bit.

"You look like a zombie," Anton continues, scrutinizing my face. "Are you even eating?"

"Yeah, yeah, I'm eating," I murmur. "How did you know I was having a slump?"

They exchange a knowing glance.

"Well, you didn't come surfing, you moron. We had two theories: either you were depressed, or you'd been abducted by aliens."

"I could also have been ill."

Anton laughs his thigh off.

"You betcha. I saw you surfing that wave with a high fever. You were half dead and still gliding through the water. So, as good friends, we figured you must have something to confide in us. And do you?"

I'm not one to shout mayday when things aren't going well...

I usually keep everything to myself and then that's it. I don't seek help in any way.

"Yeah, maybe so. Well... let's just say I had a history and..."

"Wait, with that chick you were into? Was it?"

"Yeah, you can let me finish my st..."

"Derek and I even thought you were set!"

"Listen," intervenes Derek, rising to his feet. "We're not going to leave you moping on your couch. We're going out. It's Saturday, you can't stay here when we could be surfing."

I look at them, hesitant. Part of me just wants to be left alone with my thoughts and regrets, but the other part knows that locking myself away will only make things worse.

"I don't know, I..."

"No, but," adds Anton.

"Okay," I finally sigh. "Let's go surfing."

They burst out in delight, happy to see me accept their invitation. We quickly pack up and head for the beach. On the way, I try to concentrate on the conversation, but my thoughts keep drifting.

By the time we reach the beach, I'm feeling a little better. The sea air, the sound of the waves, the feel of the sand beneath my feet... everything helps to soothe my troubled mind. I watch Anton and Derek warming up, their laughter and carefree attitude making me smile in spite of myself.

Once in the water, I give in to the feeling of freedom that surfing brings. Every wave is a challenge, a chance to focus on the moment rather than my worries. I feel alive again, at least temporarily.

When we've finished, the three of us sit on the beach with a beer in hand. These are the simple pleasures that make me forget, for a moment, that my life is falling apart. Between Elena leaving and Betty regaining control over me... nothing's going right.

"Okay, come on. We've never seen you like this."

"Not even when you split up with Betty," adds Anton. "Remember that? He was pretty happy then, our Matthew. He'd got his freedom back, the good doggie."

"Shut up," I growl.

To wash away the affront, I take a sip of beer, then stare out at the ocean.

Well, he's not entirely wrong. The day Betty and I parted was, so to speak, one of the happiest days of my life. I didn't realize it at first, but then everything became clear the very next day. I had regained a part of myself that had been missing for a long time.

"Are you going to tell us what happened?"

I take a deep breath, gather my courage and tell them the whole story. Without leaving out a single detail. Especially about my cowardice. Their eyes are as round as marbles and, for once, they don't even interrupt me when I'm talking - which is rare!

"That's it, then. You know everything," I confess.

Not one of them speaks up. They even seem to be avoiding the conversation with their sidelong glances.

"What's wrong? What the hell is wrong with you?"

"Nothing, nothing... it's just that... wow, you really didn't nail it!" says Derek.

If it was to hear me say that, eh...

"And do you love her?" asks Anton.

No sooner does he say these words than my heart starts beating a mile a minute. Do I love Elena? It's hard to say. I love her skin, her smell, her softness, the words we exchanged, but also the fact that our conversations could do without words. It was really something precious.

I think of all the times we've been together, the chemistry between us, the way she made me feel alive.

"I don't know, man," I finally say. "I know I feel something strong for her, something I haven't felt in a long time. But to call it love..."

Derek taps me on the shoulder in a show of support.

"You know, sometimes you don't realize what you've got until you've lost it."

His words resonate with me. That's exactly how I feel. I may have lost something precious with Elena, something I may never find again in someone else. Except I didn't realize it at the time.

"Maybe you should try to see her again, talk to her," suggests Anton. "You can't stay like this, moping around. This isn't you."

I nod, knowing he's right. But there's a part of me that's afraid of confrontation, afraid of what Elena might say to me.

After all, I've betrayed her, and she has every reason in the world never to want to speak to me again.

"I'll think about it," I say, "but deep down I know it's the right thing to do."

I have to find a way to make amends with Elena, to repair the damage I've caused. Nothing ventured, nothing gained, right?

Night falls slowly on the beach, and we stay there for a while. I watch the waves break on the shore, wondering what the future holds. I've made a mistake, that's for sure, but maybe it's not too late to correct it. Maybe there's still a chance for Elena and me.

"What do you recommend?" I finally ask. "I have no idea how to go about it."

Once again, my two friends look surprised.

"You're getting stranger and stranger! You, Matthew Anderson, don't know how to do it with a girl?" laughs, Derek.

"Well, listen, I've got a plan..." says Anton. "But you've got to listen to me to the letter and trust me, okay?"

18

Elena

Text message. From... Matthew? It's Sunday and I wasn't expecting this. I'm torn between anger and relief. I haven't seen him for so long. I haven't heard from him either, so maybe this message is a sign. My heart is pounding. If Kate were next to me, I'd probably ask her to type the answer for me, because I'm scared.

*We need to talk

It has the merit of being clear. Brief, but clear. What can I say to that?

I start: "Yes, that's for sure." No, that's totally lame. He'll think I'm super pissed off.

At the same time, I'm super pissed off!

OK, I'll erase my previous answer and start again: "I don't feel like talking to you!" No, I don't. Of course I want to talk to him. I want explanations and I can't miss this opportunity. What a bastard! He's still got me, even after everything he's done.

Mustang...

I tap my phone, hesitating, my finger hanging over the screen. I need to say something, to answer, but what? Every word seems too little or too 'too much'. I feel I'm still under his influence, despite my anger and determination to move on.

Finally, I type :

* Talk about what, exactly?

It's neutral, direct, but it leaves the door open for him to explain himself. I want to see what he has to say, even if part of me fears being hurt again by his words. Maybe Kate would advise against it, but Kate isn't here. Besides, I told her I wanted a meeting of the... severe kind.

I sit there, phone in hand, waiting for his answer. The seconds stretch into minutes, and each tick of the clock echoes in my head like a reminder of the tension inside me.

I hate myself for being so impatient.

The notification arrives, vibrating my phone and startling me. Matthew replies:

* I know I've made a mistake. I'd like to apologize in person. Tomorrow?

My heart is tightening. I'm going to have to face everything I've tried to put behind me these past few weeks. But on the other hand, I need to close this story, need to understand too, to know why he did what he did. Even if I know what it meant for him, of course. But to my detriment!

Everything could have been so different...

* Where and what time?

* I'll pick you up. This is a surprise. Let's say... 3 p.m.

A surprise? He's got a nerve. After what he did to me, I

think the least he could do is tell me what I'm getting into.

I'm both skeptical and curious. What is he up to? Is it a good idea to let myself be drawn into the unknown with him?

I put down my phone and lie back, staring at the ceiling. Tomorrow I'll see Matthew and maybe I'll get some answers. I try to prepare myself mentally for this meeting, promising myself to stay strong, not to let emotions overwhelm me. No matter what happens. I don't want to lose my nerve again. That wouldn't be good for me.

I spend most of the night thinking about it. Reading his message over and over again. Wondering what he could possibly want with me, and boy, am I starting to understand what Kate was talking about when she asked me if there were any flame-retardant panties! I don't know why, but Matthew always has power over me. He exerts a pressure I can't define. I'm not even with him yet and I can already feel him staring at me, as if he were there.

★ ★ ★

3:09p.m. The Mustang pulls up outside my house and my heart is beating a mile a minute. I've been preparing all morning. I've even rehearsed a little speech I've learned, because I don't want to screw up. I have the opportunity to spend some time with him and, above all, to get some explanations.

Now's not the time to screw up, girl.

I prepared myself. As I rarely do. Almost more than for a job interview or an oral exam.

I'm walking down the stairs to the lobby of my building and my legs feel like they weigh a ton. I feel so anxious. I'd rather slip through the floorboards right now and disappear forever.

Matthew Anderson, the man who broke me a week ago, at most... and I'm about to see him again. Still, you could say I'm a complete moron.

I approach the door slowly, my breathing slightly choked with anxiety. Matthew stands there, leaning against his Mustang, looking both confident and uncertain. He's wearing a navy-blue linen shirt, slightly open at the collar, revealing a fraction of his tanned skin. His jeans are fitted and show off his athletic figure. His hair is slightly mussed, giving him a casual but well-groomed look.

He looks at me and I can see a glimmer of hope mixed with concern in his eyes. His shoes, simple but elegant sneakers, complete his casual look. He seems to have made an effort, while remaining true to his style.

I stop a few steps away from him, my heart racing. This is the moment of truth. I take a deep breath, trying to gather my courage and determination. I'm ready to hear what he has to say, but also ready to defend myself, to hold my ground.

The moment of confrontation has arrived.

"Hi, there."

"Hello Elena."

Matthew looks at me intensely, his blue eyes reflecting a complex emotion I can't quite decipher. He remains silent, as if measuring the importance of this moment between us. His gaze briefly roams across my face, perhaps trying to read my thoughts, my feelings.

Don't let it show, Elena. Poker face first, as Lady Gaga would say[6].

Then, without a word, he opens the passenger door with nonchalant elegance - a gesture that seems so natural to him. And with a wave of his hand, he invites me to take my place inside. He remains serious. Impassive. Seductive. Damn, he's handsome when he's being mysterious and I'm falling for it

6 *Poker face is a Lady Gaga song. It's about keeping a poker face without the slightest emotion.*

like a fool. I feel like I'm 18.

I approach the car, hesitant, but finally climb aboard. Matthew gently closes the door behind me, then settles behind the wheel. His gaze is still fixed on the road ahead, as if he's trying to avoid mine. The tension is palpable, but there's also a kind of silent respect in his demeanor. I don't know how to interpret this situation. I expected anything but this.

The car starts up slowly, pulling away from my apartment. Matthew remains silent, letting the road and the soft music in the background fill the space between us. I feel both intrigued and anxious, wondering where he's taking me and what he plans to say or do.

"Are you... going to talk, or...?"

It's a suspended moment, a moment when anything can happen, and I feel my heart pounding in my chest in anticipation of what's to come.

My breathing quickens. What's he got in mind?

"At first, I intended to," he admits, without looking away from the road. "But... then I remembered that between you and me, there was no need for words."

I swallow. Impossible to answer anything.

I don't want to admit that I'm under his spell. And shit...

The car continues on its way, moving away from the busy city streets towards an unknown destination. The silence thickens, every second seems to stretch out. I watch him from time to time, trying to decipher what's going on behind his concentrated gaze.

Finally, the Mustang slows down and stops on a deserted beach spot, far from the hustle and bustle of the city.

"Where are we?"

"I've already told you about my favorite spots, haven't I? Well... this is one of them. There's the one I come to surf with my friends, which I've already shown you. And then there's this one which is more... a place of recollection, for me. When I'm here, I feel good."

"And... what's all this?" I ask, pointing to a pile of stuff he's tucked under his arm, along with a tall bag shaped like a surfboard.

"I hope you're not planning to murder me, dissolve me in soda ash and bury me on this beach," I continue.

Matthew smiles, then we start walking on the warm sand.

"That, my dear, is groceries, namely: cheap beers, self-made sandwiches, a bouquet of flowers, a surfboard and a great book of poems I love. It's Charles Bukowski[7]."

Ha, well done! Really well done.

"I thought we were going to talk. I'm... I'm waiting for an explanation, Matthew."

"We'll talk," he replies softly, placing all the equipment on the sand. "But first I wanted to create the right environment, a place where we could be ourselves, without pressure."

We sit down on the sand, facing the ocean. Matthew brings out the sandwiches, then hands me one. I take it, still a little wary, but I can't deny that the place is beautiful and soothing.

He opens a beer and holds it out to me. Our hands brush lightly and I feel a spark, a memory of what brought us together in the first place, pass between us. I take the beer, our eyes meet and I see a sincerity, a vulnerability I hadn't seen before in him.

"First of all, I want to apologize, Elena. For everything. I should never have put you in such a situation. I acted out of fear and selfishness, and I deeply regret what I did."

His voice is soft, but full of emotion. I listen, trying to keep my heart closed, but it's difficult. Matthew's words, the ocean, all gradually soften my anger.

"I've thought about you every day since," he continues. "I

---

7 *German-born American writer of novels, short stories and poetry.*

don't know if I can fix what I've broken, but I want to try. I want you to know that you mean more to me than I ever imagined. More than a job, or the idea of taking a van on an adventure.

I remain silent, absorbing his words. Part of me wants to shout at him, to tell him how much he's hurt me, but another part is touched by his gesture, by his sincere words.

"I... I don't know what to say, Matthew. You really hurt me."

He nods.

"I know you don't. And I understand if you don't want anything to do with me. I just wanted you to know the truth. I wanted, maybe before you didn't want to talk to me anymore, to show you what I'm passionate about above all else. What makes me feel really... really free, you know?"

"You mean surfing?"

A spark of mischief runs through his eyes.

"Precisely. As far as you're concerned, Elena, I... I acted like a fool and in the end, I lost everything. But you should know that it's not all over, either."

I raise an eyebrow. What's he talking about?

Matthew bows his head, then sighs heavily.

"I... I worked it out, Elena."

"How?"

"Betty wants to keep me at the bookstore no matter what. She knows it won't last long without me. Besides, she wants me around all the time, so... well, you get the idea of what kind of woman she is, I guess. So... I offered her a deal she can't refuse."

Now I'm more and more intrigued. Silent, I drink in his words.

"She's agreed to take you back and wipe the slate clean."

"Wait, wait," I cut him off. "What are you saying?"

"Well, that you'll be able to become a department manager,

that your hours will be shorter, that you'll be better paid..."

I plant my gaze in his, but he immediately avoids it.

"In exchange for what, exactly?"

"Elena... That's all you need to know."

"Matthew, I want to know. What did you offer her?"

"It was your dream to work in a bookstore, wasn't it? You want to make a life here too and I've ruined it. I had no right to do that. I've made amends and that's all that matters."

I shake my head.

"Absolutely not. You... you matter too."

"Don't talk nonsense. I've spoken to Betty and she's agreed. Tomorrow... you can come back to the bookstore if you like and I, well, I'll still be there. But I'll be transferred to another department and I won't be your... direct superior, if you know what I mean. But I'll be staying for an extended period of time. I'm going to make a very long-term commitment to her. That's the deal."

His freedom... against my reinstatement? In short, his dream against mine.

I'm stunned. To sacrifice his freedom, his dream, to allow me to realize mine? It's an incredible gesture, but at the same time, it hurts my heart. I can't accept such a sacrifice. For me, it's a great opportunity to work with books and continue writing, but for Matthew, it's more than *that*.

"Matthew, I... I can't accept this," I whisper in a voice choked with emotion.

He looks at me, his eyes reflecting the same sadness I feel.

"It's already done, Elena. It was the only way. I couldn't let you pay for my mistakes. This is my way of making amends, of giving you back what I took from you. I told Betty I'd do it, so..."

I feel tears welling up in my eyes. It's a noble gesture, but so painful. The thought of him sacrificing himself for me makes me feel even guiltier.

"But Matthew, what about you? What about your dreams? What about your future? You told me about your van, your idea of crisscrossing the West Coast..."

He shrugs, then gives me a smile.

"My dreams? They don't really matter now. What matters is that you have a chance to make yours come true. Mine can wait."

I shake my head, feeling torn between gratitude and anguish. How can I be happy to go back to work, knowing it's at the cost of her happiness?

And then, finally, shit! Losing this job was a good kick in the ass, after all.

"I can't accept that, Matthew. It just isn't fair. There's got to be another way."

He sighs and runs a hand through his hair, visibly frustrated.

"Elena, it's done. I've made my decision. You don't have to feel guilty. It's my choice. Not yours."

I look out at the ocean, lost in thought. I'm torn between the desire to reclaim my place at the bookstore and the guilt of knowing it's at Matthew's expense. I wonder if I'll ever be able to forgive myself, or him, for this choice.

Safety or a leap into the void?

You only live once.

"In the meantime, since I'm about to lose my freedom, I wanted to savor it with you. Would you mind if I took a dip in the ocean and enjoyed the waves? I think I'd like to teach you a thing or two about surfing."

"About?... But... I don't even have a bathing suit, and..."

At this point, Matthew smiles, then pulls out a swimsuit from the bag of belongings he's brought with him.

"I thought you'd like it, and then I was pretty sure you'd

195

arrived in San Francisco without a swimsuit."

It's a one-piece in navy blue, with thin straps and a swimmer's back. The fabric seems of good quality, soft to the touch, and there are small touches of white color along the edges.

All right, he's clearly planned ahead.

I remain silent for a moment, looking at Matthew, then at the surfboard. I've never surfed in my life, and the idea is both exciting and frightening. But he's right, life is for living, for taking risks, for experimenting.

"You had it all figured out, didn't you?"

I see his charming smile again.

"Down to the last detail. So, will you try it on? I'll turn around, I promise. Although, between you and me... we've already seen everything there is to see."

He's not wrong, but still. Once I'm changed - behind a towel - Matthew looks delighted.

"Okay," I finally agree. "Show me how it's done."

Matthew smiles, his eyes shining with a gleam I haven't seen in a long time. He seems almost relieved, as if he's been waiting for this moment all his life.

"Perfect. So, let's start with the basics."

He guides me to the board, explaining basic surfing techniques. His voice is calm, patient, and I listen attentively, trying to absorb every word, every piece of advice. He shows me how to stand on the board, how to row with my arms, how to stand up.

"Don't be afraid of falling," he laughs. "That's part of the game. The important thing is to get up and try again."

I nod, and together we head for the water. The ocean is gentle and welcoming, the waves punctuating our progress. Matthew stays by my side, encouraging me, guiding me. Every time I fall, he helps me up, putting me back in the saddle with infinite patience. He's even more handsome when he's in the water. His body seems even more sculpted, as the drops of water glide over his tanned skin. He's wearing black swim shorts that fit his athletic figure perfectly. He's a real looker.

When he holds my hand to help me find my balance on the board, I feel a warmth spreading through me, an attraction that goes beyond the physical. He's handsome, yes, but it's the passion in his eyes, his commitment to every movement, that touches me the most. He shares a piece of his world with me, and I can't help but feel connected to him in a new and profound way.

After several attempts, I finally manage to stand up on the board, gliding through the water with an incredible sense of freedom. I laugh, the splashes of salt water refreshing my face, and feel a sense of accomplishment wash over me.

"You're doing great!" he says. "Keep it up!"

That's all it took for me to lose my balance and fall. But always with a great burst of laughter.

Matthew applauds me from his own board, a broad smile on his face. I feel alive, free, far from the complications of everyday life. It's a moment of pure joy, a suspended moment in time when nothing else matters.

As the sun begins to set, tinting the sky orange and pink, we return to the beach.

I'm so happy. The adrenalin is still coursing through my veins.

He can't give it up.

Matthew is a grouch and when he's in the water, all that evaporates. He exudes joy.

I can't take that from him... He'd be willing to... sacrifice everything he loves... for me.

That's not an option. I have to find another solution. I have to tell him that, in the end, what I want is to try my luck elsewhere. I want to try to become the author I've always dreamed

197

of being. And I don't mind finding a food job on the side.

We settle down on the warm sand, then Matthew pulls out his book of poetry, which we both start to read. It's terribly *too much*, but also terribly romantic. Even so, it's effective, because I'm snuggled up to him and, once again, I can feel us getting closer.

"Matthew..."

He looks up at me.

"No," I say.

"What are you talking about?"

"About what you told me. About your position at the bookstore, etc. That's a no. I don't want you to sacrifice yourself for me."

He puts the book down, then frowns.

"But..."

"Don't say anything. Please don't say anything. I've found myself a bit these last few weeks. I, too, am passionate about letters. Beautiful letters. I've started writing again. I've rediscovered that taste. OK, it's not safe at all. OK, I'll certainly have to find a job on the side; otherwise I won't make it, but it doesn't matter. It's not a problem. I'm willing to give it a go. Anyway," I continue, "I'm not coming back. I'm happy with what I've written this week and I'm not going to give up. I'm going to fight. I've been thinking about it for years, writing in my corner. I just... I want it to happen, you know? I want it to happen."

Matthew looks worried but, in the end, smiles.

"Would you let me read what you write?"

"I... I... well, you're a great lover of literature, I think it would terrify me, you know?"

"Here's a thought. You might need some help if you're going to do this. So, you're going to come to the event we've organized. Some of the authors will be there. Maybe they could read what you've done, couldn't they? Or give you some tips on how to get into the business?

I open my eyes wide. Oh, boy, what he's offering me is huge, but then again, it's very intimidating.

"Are you serious? Do you think it could do it?"

"But of course! Don't doubt yourself so much. I'm sure what you write is great! Besides, we organized this event together, didn't we?"

"Yes, b-but..."

Matthew takes my hand and I shiver.

"Elena... please. Don't hide what you're doing from the world. If it sucks, I promise, I'll tell you."

At least it's honest.

And there we stay, snuggled up together, until the sun slowly declines.

"I... I'd really like you to forgive me. I'm ready to make any sacrifice for you," he breathes softly.

He has a sad look on his face. Fuck, I really want to kiss him. After an afternoon of surfing, his mouth must have a slight salty taste that I crave.

"Matthew, I... I forgive you" I say, my voice trembling with emotion. "I know you made a mistake, but I can also see that you're sincere in your remorse. I can't condemn you for this... It's not possible."

He looks at me, relieved, and a shy smile appears on his lips.

"Thank you, Elena. It means the world to me. It really does."

The sunset paints the sky a vivid pink and orange, creating the perfect setting for this moment. Matthew approaches slowly, and I feel my heart beating faster. He's there, in front of me, with that intensity that's always drawn me in, that depth that captivates me.

He places his hand gently on my cheek, then his eyes plunge into mine. I lose myself in his gaze, the warmth of his hand against my skin.

"Elena," he murmurs.

And then he kisses me. It's a soft, tender kiss, full of emotion. A kiss that seems to mend some of the pain, some of the rift between us. It's a kiss that speaks of promise, of hope, of second chances. I'm rocked.

I respond to his kiss, letting myself be carried away by the magic of the moment. The world around us fades away, there's just him and me, the sound of the waves, and the softness of the sunset.

It's the most beautiful kiss in the world, in the most beautiful place in the world. For a moment, everything is perfect.

19

Elena

My heart is pounding as I pull up in front of the bookstore. The big night. It's finally here. I didn't think I'd ever get there again. For me... it was ancient history. Yet I have the beginnings of a manuscript pressed firmly against my chest. I hold it against me as if it were a baby - although I'd make a terrible mother, because I'd probably be smothering it with all my might!

"Calm down," Matthew says. "It's going to be okay, I promise."

And he's standing next to me. He looks like he's never been so serene in his life.

He grabs one of my hands and slips it into his. It's so unexpected.

We could be seen.

But I don't think he cares. This time, it doesn't really matter to him. The big night is here. It's about to start and we look like a couple. He's nuts. Fuck, this guy's crazy and he's driving me crazy. If someone catches us... we're screwed. Well, mostly him, since I'm already fired and I can't imagine the worst that could happen to me right now.

We walk through the door of the bookstore together, hand in hand. The interior is alive with energy and conversation. I feel a little involved, because I've also participated in the creation of this moment. Authors, publishers, there's a bit of everything here. Matthew has seen the big picture, I see. When I was fired, he was forced to take over the project with Betty, and she didn't do things by halves either.

"It's not... quite what we had in mind, is it?"

"And no," he retorts, laughing. "But, on the other hand, who cares, right? It's all about Betty now."

The light is subdued, creating a warm and welcoming atmosphere. Stacks of carefully arranged books adorn every corner, and I can even see my former work colleagues bustling about. The stage, meanwhile, is set for literary readings and discussions. Even if it's a lot more ambitious than we originally imagined, there's no doubt that this event will be a real success. Betty has thought big, and... perhaps that's just as well.

"Well, come on, I'll introduce you."

Suddenly, a wave of panic sweeps over me and I stiffen.

"Introduce... me? But wait... to... to whom...?"

"To authors. Or... publishers, whatever. Anyway, I'll make sure you get noticed, Woodstock."

It reminds me of our early days. Except this time, Mustang is much more attentive.

"Are you sure about this? Seems a little fast to me, and..."

"Ahhh, there you are at last!" says Kate as she approaches us. "Say, Matthew, it's about time. Were you going to wait for the wine to turn to vinegar before you arrived?"

He looks up at the ceiling.

"Yes, well, it's not the delay of my life either, is it?"

"Fifteen minutes! In the life of an author, or a guy who reads poetry while surfing, that's nothing. But in the life of a publisher..."

I blush. So, he told her. She knows all about the beach, the publisher, the authors and everything?

"You... she knows everything?" I stammer.

Kate nods with satisfaction.

"You don't think that idiot would have thought of all that without me, do you?"

I give Matthew a tender look. I know that anyone would say that he hasn't made the effort to think about all these things himself, but I see the reality in a different way: he dared to ask Kate, my best friend, to help him, even if it meant taking a beating. Because I don't doubt for a moment that she made him regret everything that happened - and that he had to pay for it a hundredfold. It must have been hard for her to keep the surprise intact. But the result is there for all to see: I'm delighted.

Matthew guides me through the crowd, introducing me to some familiar and some new faces. His embrace is firm, re-assuring. I can feel the curious glances following us, but he doesn't seem to mind. He's focused, almost as if he had a specific goal in mind.

"Are you ready?" he asks, as he leads me towards a small group of authors.

I nod, even though my stomach is in knots. This is a milestone, a step towards realizing my dream. I look at the faces around me, feeling the excitement building.

In fact, I'm not ready at all. But never mind... I've got both feet in it now.

One of the authors, a friendly-looking man with round glasses, smiles warmly at me as Matthew introduces me.

"Elena, it's a pleasure to meet you. Matthew has told me a lot about you and your project."

I'm surprised, but pleasantly so. Matthew really supports me, more than I'd imagined.

How could he even mention my project? He doesn't even know about it! Oh, dear... he made it up. That'll be a shame.

203

I'm biting my nails in anticipation. I have NO idea how to stand. Matthew, on the other hand, looks calm and relaxed, as usual. He grabs a glass that a waiter brings on a tray, then hands it to me - before grabbing one, too.

How can he be so relaxed?

"Elena was wondering if you could take a look at her manuscript," says Matthew.

Holy shit. It's like I'm breaking the ice, but he's settling down. This isn't an elephant-in-a-china-shop approach, this is the herd coming in. He's completely nuts!

"Of course!"

And what's worse, it works.

"Thank you" I retort, a little intimidated. "I hope you like what I've written."

The author nods and takes the manuscript I hand him. He begins to leaf through it with a very serious air. Matthew squeezes my hand tighter in a silent show of support. Whatever happens next, I know I've taken a crucial step, with him by my side.

Suddenly, I see her. Oh, no... She was the only thing left to ruin everything. Of course, it was a foregone conclusion that I'd run into her.

Betty...

Her eyes run over Matthew and me. I try to untangle my fingers from those of my partner, who quickly understands the situation. Their eyes meet, then the handsome blond grabs my hand again. Proudly. Shamelessly. As if it had always been natural.

"What the hell are you doing?"

"I assert myself. I don't have to live a lie or hide. I already made that mistake once, with you. I'm not going to make it again."

"You're going to have a hell of a time here if you insist on this."

"So be it. No problem for me"

Betty obviously wants to talk to him. She beckons Matthew to come closer.

"Can you give me a second?" he asks.

Without another word, I nod. Oh, boy, do I feel sick to my stomach.

★ ★ ★

Matthew

Betty takes me into her office as we had agreed beforehand.

"What do you want?" I say. "I don't think I'm supposed to report to you tonight."

Actually, a little bit, since I'm organizing the evening with her and I'm working right now. But I don't care. It's not important to me anymore. I've realized that there's a lot more to it than breaking free from Betty's chains. She won't be able to put the leash back around my neck. No matter how hard she tries.

Betty's office is as impeccable and controlled as her appearance. As usual. She clearly prefers to talk to people in this place, because she knows she has home-court advantage. But I'm not going to let that happen. Not again. I won't let it happen. She sits behind her desk, the subdued light accentuating the sharp features of her face. Her eyes stare at me, a mixture of cold anger and calculation.

I know her when she's like that. It doesn't bode well. But beyond the intimidation and the threat: what can she really do against me?

"Matthew" she begins, her voice measured but razor-sharp. "What do you think you're doing, showing off like this? You know the consequences, don't you?"

I remain standing, refusing to sit down. I've made up my mind, I'm not backing down. I can't let Betty dictate my life, not this time. I've got to do this. For Elena. She deserves it. I think we can both be happy.

"I'm doing what I should have done a long time ago. I've had enough of playing by your rules."

She grits her teeth, her mask of control cracking slightly. I can see the anger boiling inside her, but she holds back, still maintaining a facade of calm.

"You owe me everything, Matthew. Your career, your position here... everything. And you betray that for... what? A fling?"

"It's not a fling," I retort. "Elena is much more than that."

She giggles, as if I've just said something outrageous.

"Oh, please stop making a fool of yourself, poor thing. It's so unlike you. Ray told me you were seeing her, outside the bookstore. I thought I made that clear."

I tilt my head to the side with a wry smile. Oh, from what I can see, he doesn't like it at all, but... I don't care. It's not my problem anymore. It's amazing how... light everything can seem when you start not caring.

"So what?"

"You don't respect our conditions."

I raise my index finger in protest.

"I'll stop you right there. On the contrary, our conditions were extremely clear: you'd get Elena back here and I'd work

206

in the bookstore without thinking of leaving. But that's all. And I remind you that they're no longer valid, since Elena hasn't wanted to come back. So, there's no question of not being able to see her. If I want to take her to the bookstore, I'll take her to the bookstore. If I want to have ice cream with her, it's the same thing. You just don't get it, do you? I don't think you get it, but... you're nothing to me anymore. You're just my boss and nothing else. And Elena and I owe you nothing."

Betty's anger turns into a mixture of surprise and restrained fury. She rises abruptly, her movements almost mechanical, and I can almost hear the gears of her calculating mind turning at full speed.

"So that's how it is? You think you're strong enough to challenge my authority?"

Her voice is calm, but every word is laden with a veiled threat. She moves towards me, but I don't back down. I've made up my mind and I'm sticking to it.

"I'm not challenging your authority. I'm simply reclaiming my personal freedom. You can't control every aspect of my life."

She stares at me, her eyes searching mine, looking for a flaw, a sign of weakness. But I give her none. No satisfaction for her this time. I'll stand firm.

"Do you realize you're playing with fire? You could lose everything. I could fire you!"

"I've already lost everything once," I retort. "I've got nothing left to lose. It's still just a job, Betty."

If I reduce the value of my work at the bookstore, she has no hold on me. I play it tactically, because yes, I still need this job, but she doesn't have to know that.

There's a moment of palpable tension, a silent face-off where each measures the other. Finally, Betty takes a step back, as if she's just made a decision.

"Is she worth it? This girl has nothing, no stature. She's banal, like a lot of other women you meet on the street every day. And you do you fall for her?"

I should be getting angry. I should be getting offended and railing against everything she's just said about Elena, but instead, I'm smiling.

"What's so funny?" she asks with a hint of annoyance in her voice.

"You've got it all wrong. She's the opposite. She's what you'll never be. Passionate. A real one."

Betty tensed up, every word seeming to hit her like an arrow. Her face hardens, betraying a cold rage bubbling beneath her usually controlled surface.

"You dare to compare me to that... girl? You know very well that without me, you're nothing in this literary world. So, I'm going to repeat myself, but: are you ready to sacrifice everything for a fling?"

Her question is tinged with contempt, but I don't let it throw me. I know her attempts to throw me off balance, to make me doubt. But this time, I'm certain of my feelings, of my choice.

"This is more than a fling, Betty. This is the first time in a long time that I really feel alive. And that's because of her."

Betty shakes her head, a bitter laugh escaping her lips.

"You'll be back, Matthew. They always do."

I stand up, ready to leave his office. His power over me fades, dissipates like fog in the sun.

"Maybe the others come back, but not me. I've found something far more precious than anything you've ever offered me or can offer me."

She's bubbling inside. I see it and rejoice. She doesn't know how much.

"Will you let me get back to our guests? After all, I do work here, don't I?"

"You're completely unprofessional."

I raise an eyebrow.

"Is that so? Well, the evening's going swimmingly so... what's not working for you, Betty?"

"Elena," she squeaks. "She doesn't belong here."

I shrug mockingly.

"She has the right to come to the bookstore. She's a customer like any other. And you're not one to turn away customers, are you?"

Once again, Betty seems to be seething. I'm sure she's on the verge of exploding. Her fingernails are almost scratching the desk, she's so angry. It won't be long before she starts screaming, and that's extremely rare. Maybe I'll be treated to that kind of intense rage again? I can't wait to find out.

"She's not just a customer. She's your girlfriend."

"But there's nothing to stop me bringing her here, is there? She'll probably meet me after work, every day. And maybe we'll make out on the sidewalk. All this, of course, while staying outside the bookstore door because, you see, I wouldn't want to disturb your little peace and quiet."

"I see right through you, Matthew. You can't win. Not with me."

"You think so? I think I've already won. You just can't stand to see me with another woman on a daily basis. And all you have to threaten me with is this job, but I can still leave. Except that if I leave, your bookstore goes out of business. So, business or self-respect first? What an insoluble situation..."

"You little son of a..."

What a joy to see that everything she's built as a chain around me is melting and dissipating. She's no longer holding me. There's nothing left to hold me back, one way or another. If I even decide to give up this job, then I'm completely free. I won't have any money left in the immediate future to refurbish my van. But... then what? I'll be rid of everything that weighs me down in the world. I'll also be able to find a job that's just for food. Basically, I don't care, as long as I can live the way I want.

She's used to controlling everything and everyone around her, but this time I'm determined not to give in.

"Matthew, do you realize what you're doing? You can't just drop everything for... for a girl! You can't be that detached," she squeaks. "It's got to be a bluff."

His voice is full of contempt, but I remain unmoved. I've already made up my mind. It's a choice between my freedom and remaining in his grip. And I've chosen freedom.

"My choice is made, Betty. I'm quitting."

Her eyes widen in surprise at my firmness.

"You can't do this to me!"

There's a hint of desperation in his voice, but it's too late. I'm tired of playing by his rules, tired of feeling trapped. I want to spread my wings and fly.

"I have to think about myself, about what I really want in life. And today, I don't owe you anything."

She walks towards me, her footsteps echoing on the wooden floor.

"You're going to lose everything, Matthew. You're going to regret this decision."

I shake my head, a sad smile on my lips.

"No, Betty. I'm getting more out of this than you think. This is my chance to start something new, something real."

She stands there, helpless, as I head for the door. I can feel her anger and frustration, but I don't turn around.

"Matthew, you're going to regret this! You won't find anything better than what I offered you!"

But her words no longer reach me. I am free. Free from

Betty, free from the bookstore, free to pursue my own life. To be with Elena without hindrance... to really be with her. With nothing but her and me, if she wants. And if she wants to live this crazy adventure with me.

As I leave her office, I find Elena waiting for me, worried. I take her hand, a liberating smile on my lips.

"It's over," I say. I'm free. "I've just resigned."

In return, she smiles at me.

"I thought that..."

"That my dream should force me to put up with such a self-important woman and forget who I really am? No, I've thought it through, and it's the best decision I've made in leaving. I'll find another job until I finish fixing up my van, and besides, as much as I like this bookstore, I don't like who's running it."

I grab her hands and place a kiss on her lips.

"And... I've always dreamed of having someone accompany me, to travel the West Coast. What do you say?" I say with a smile.

Epilogue
Elena

It's so rushed and so crazy that I can't resist for a moment. Me, embarking on such a crazy adventure? After all, why not? And with Matthew, too.

However, there are several logistical issues to consider.

The first: I'm a little bit broke. But first things first. I've got a little job waiting for me, which will allow me to put a bit of money aside for the big departure.

The second, the van still needs a few repairs, but that's without counting on Matthew's loyal friends: Anton and Derek. These two put in a lot of elbow grease and even invested a few dollars in the repairs. And then, to mark Matthew's farewell party, a fundraiser was organized at the bookstore, with everyone pitching in - well, except Betty and Ray.

Matthew was thinking of selling his Mustang, but I talked him out of it. After all, the car has sentimental value for me now too! Anton will look after it when we're on the road, and he's promised to take good care of it. As for Matt's apartment, he'll be subletting it while we're away to ensure a regular nest egg. As for me, I've stored my meagre belongings in a storage unit, and that's fine by me!

The result? We spend most of our time on the beach, soaking up the sun and refurbishing the old van, in preparation for our departure for the West Coast. In between, we sip beers with friends and go surfing, while doing odd jobs that keep us going.

That's happiness, plain and simple.

"So it's safe?" says Kate, clinking her bottle against mine.

I glance in the direction of Matthew, who is washing the windshield with his two friends.

"Yeah. It sure is. I don't think it's ever been more so."

"You've just arrived in San Francisco and a few months later, you're off with your ex-boss on an adventure to the West Coast of the United States. And you thought I was the crazy one."

I still think so.

"Wow, nice," exclaims Travis as he joins us on the beach and notices the van. "So, is this the thing?"

"No, 'the thing,' as you call it, is what Elena calls Matthew's penis. But this is the van, yes."

They both burst out laughing and I don't know where to stand, as usual. At least she hasn't lost that crude way of expressing herself. That would have been almost... disappointing.

"And to think he was such a jerk to you in the first place," she murmurs. "What was it you used to call him?"

Just thinking about it brings a smile to my face.

"Mustang."

"Ahhh, yes, that's it! Mustang and Woodstock."

That's what we had engraved on the back of the van.

We burst out laughing, the sound mixing with the sound of the waves and the laughter of our friends. It's a perfect moment, one of those when everything seems to align.

Matthew comes towards us, a radiant smile lighting up his face. He looks more relaxed, happier than ever. His hair is a mess from the wind, and his eyes shine with that sparkle that had drawn me in from day one.

"So, ready for the adventure of a lifetime?" he asks, sitting down next to me.

I nod, my heart full of excitement and a little nervousness.

"More than ever," I say. "It's crazy, but I'm ready to jump into the void with you."

Matthew takes my hand, squeezing it gently.

"We're about to experience something incredible, Elena. I can feel it. It's a new page, a new beginning for both of us."

"Haem... looks like I'll be leaving you to it," Kate sneers. "Maybe you need some privacy."

I look around me, at our friends bustling around the van, at the blue sky and ocean stretching as far as the eye can see. It all seems so unreal, like a daydream.

"And Betty, she hasn't called you back since?"

Matthew shrugs, a quiet smile on his lips.

"No, she hasn't. She's still searching for her pride under the bookstore shelves. We're going to get away from it all, explore, live, and write our own story."

I'm overcome by a sense of freedom and adventure. Yes, it's risky. Yes, it's crazy, but it's exactly what I need.

I never imagined for a moment that this man I called Mustang would one day bring it to me.

When the day of departure arrives, all our friends are gathered to say goodbye. Oh, it's not final: far from it. In a few months, we'll be back, and that's fine with me. We'll just live a different life for a while. Our home will be the van. Our hobbies will be the beaches, and our activities, literature and surfing. We've already planned a rough itinerary. In addition, Matthew will give surfing lessons as he moves from beach to beach. As for me, I'll be concentrating on the rest of my manuscript.

When the engine roars to life, ready to go, I feel a twinge of nostalgia. It's a strange feeling, a mixture of excitement and nostalgia, as we leave what has been our lives for a while to venture into the unknown.

So, this is it. We're leaving for real.

I take one last look at San Francisco, at the familiar faces waving at us, and feel that this is the end of one chapter and the beginning of another. Matthew is by my side, his arm around my shoulders, and I feel incredibly lucky to have him with me.

My thoughts fly to my friends, and I smile softly.

I hope Kate makes it with Travis. She deserves it!

As we hit the road, the sun sets, painting the sky in shades of pink and orange. It's beautiful, and I can't help thinking it's a sign, a good omen for our journey.

"Where are we going first?" I ask, curious about our first destination.

"South," replies Matthew. "We'll follow the coast, stopping wherever the mood takes us. There's no fixed plan, no final destination. Just us, the road and the ocean. By the way, the author I introduced you to told me he'd sent you some feedback. What did he think? I didn't dare ask you before... And since you didn't mention it..."

I can't wait to tell him all about it. I wanted to talk to him about it, but with all the preparations, we didn't have much time to sit down. And I wanted to share it with him calmly.

"Well... he loved it!" I exclaim.

"Are you kidding me? And you didn't tell me?"

"I still have secrets for you, Mustang."

Matthew smiles tenderly.

Him, the beach and my text. Now that's all that really matters to me.

"Very good, Woodstock. I'll be happy to pierce them, then."

"I don't only have secrets for you, though..."

"Ho? What else?"

The road goes by slowly, the air freshens as the sun declines, and I feel really happy.

"Yes... I have feelings too."

I see his face light up with a smile.

"That's good, because me too..."

Suddenly, he flicks on the blinker and parks the van on the side of the road, in the last rays of sunlight. He turns to me and takes my face in his warm hands.

"I love you, Elena. I think this is the best time to tell you."

I close my eyes to taste a delicious kiss.

"If the moment is perfect then... I love you too, Matthew."

Our eyes are magnetized to each other and we know very well what happens when we look at each other like that.

"What if we christened the van for a torrid embrace?" asks the handsome blond.

"You read my mind, I was going to suggest it!" I laugh against his mouth, already eager for him to pull me into the back of the car.

"At this rate, we're not even close..."

"Who cares? We've got all the time in the world!"

And no one can ever take that away from us.

Our books are also available in e-book. Find our catalog on:
https://cherry-publishing.com/en/

Subscribe to our newsletter and receive a free ebook! You'll also receive the latest updates on all of our upcoming

publications!

https://mailchi.mp/b78947827e5e/get-your-free-ebook

Editorial manager: Audrey Puech
Composition and layout: Cherry Publishing
Interior Illustrations: © Shutterstock
Cover design: Keti Matakov
Cover illustration: Keti Matakov